In the Shadow
of the Sphinx

In the Shadow of the Sphinx

Reena Puri

PARTRIDGE
A Penguin Random House Company

To order additional copies of this book, contact
Partridge India
000 800 10062 62
orders.india@partridgepublishing.com

www.partridgepublishing.com/india

CONTENTS

This book is dedicated in the memory of
my beloved mother-in-law, Shama Puri
Whereever You are
I know your blessings
Are with me.

I want to be the eagle
Soaring in the brilliant blue sky
My mind and body surrendered to the eddies of
currents
Let them guide me to a path of least resistance
I will rise up again like a Phoenix from the ashes

FOREWORD

I did not know, till a year back, that I had it in me to write a romance novel, though I had grown up on a daily diet of Mills and Boon romances during my teenage years. It just happened and has taken me more than six months to write this story.

The journey has been fraught with self-doubts and writer's block wondering whether my book would see the light of the day or was it just a whimsical hobby that would peter off.

I have finally done it and would thank all the people who have been on this journey with me.

My husband, Rajesh Puri, who has been with me each step, listening and suggesting changes and doing the difficult and time-consuming copyediting. Thank you darling for bearing up with my story narratives and the fun we had about you know what!

Subhash Misra, my dear friend who writes amazing poetry and was the first person to believe that I had written a story that should get a shot at publishing. Thank you Subhash, my book is to your credit.

My dear friend Anita Misra, thank you so much for reading the story, for your words of encouragement and valuable suggestions.

I was not sure how and what I should be doing to make sure that my book got the right launch, and I wish to thank my son, Aditya Puri, who showed me the right direction and told me to go for it.

I would also give my heartfelt thanks to my friends Anand Keswani, Pummy Vasudeva, Rajni Agarwal and many more friends, for the amazing encouragement they gave to the few excerpts that I shared with them, which made me believe that I could do a story.

CHAPTER 1

It was the same old routine, which I could probably do with my eyes shut! Of managing my home and looking after my family. Somewhere down life's road, I had lost me. It was there, emerging now and then, and yet again disappearing under the burden of an important phase of life, which needed it more than me.

Then came a point in my life when everything turned one eighty degrees!

My children were away to the University and busy with lives of their own. My husband and I were going through a midlife crisis with which we had been struggling for a long time and we decided to separate, though not legally, for a period till we could settle the crisis, in a civil and mature way.

It seemed so cold and mechanical; we had been so in love. I could not think of a moment in life without him. But then life was a bitch, throwing up surprises when you least expected them. In the last few years we had somehow made sure our children were never affected and this had taken a mental toll on me.

I just needed to get away from this traumatic situation, and prove to my own self that I was worth something.

I decided to search for me, and embarked on a solo trip to Egypt, to see and explore the land of the pyramids, that had enthralled me since my teenage days.

I had booked my self on a flexi-customized tour. Soon D-day dawned, I was rushing off to the Delhi International Airport, a little behind schedule due to sorting out the last minute glitches, that we women seem to get a high on!

This, compounded with an unexpected traffic jam and a high-on-testosterone taxi driver who weaved in and out of the traffic with madness, made sure that I was almost a nervous wreck by the time I reached the airport.

I rushed towards my airline counter with such an intense relief that I almost did not see the suitcase lying in the path, and tried in vain to get my balance, my arms akimbo trying to clutch vainly at any thing that would save me from landing in an ignoble heap on the floor.

Wow, what a fantastic start on my road to searching me!

As if in slow motion, a pair of strong arms came from behind and stalled my fall, holding me from my waist. My breath knocked out and my mouth open in a silent oh, I fell back in my savior's arms.

I heard a deep sexy voice enquire amusingly, "Lady, are you all right?" I almost died of mortification.

His tone made me look and feel like a bumbling idiot. Hardly befitting a woman embarked on a journey of finding her self!

Finding my balance, I turned around to look in to a pair of dark brooding eyes set in a strong angular face. His dark unruly hair, liberally streaked with silver, were a little on the longer side. For a man in his early fifties, he seemed to be well kept with a lean physique exuding that same quiet strength of his hands, for I was no feather weight. He was wearing faded blue denims with an off white tee and soft blue suede moccasins, with a nonchalance bordering on arrogance.

An almost cynical smile on his sensual lips belied his solicitous enquiry. For a moment, I almost thought of telling him curtly that I was fine and could he please lay his hands off from my waist.

Ashamed of being so bitchy, my innate good manners prevailed and I fumbled with my thanks. I was in a tearing hurry to get away from this magnetic stranger, who seemed to have tripped some switch in my inner being.

Without any further mishaps, I completed my boarding formalities and proceeded to the Emirates flight gate. I had a two-hour stop over at Dubai, from where I would be taking off for Cairo, safely reaching in the early evening to embark on a fortnight of adventure and self-seeking.

Finally my flight was announced and as I stood in the queue to board the plane, my heart almost skipped a beat, seeing the handsome stranger up ahead in the line for business class passengers.

I almost smirked, aha, money and attitude, well; there would be no chance of crossing path with him en flight as I was travelling in the economy class.

The three-hours-some-minute's flight ended in no time. Disembarking, my eyes searched for some one and

I mentally reprimanded myself for being a masochist and made my way through to terminal 3 for my onward flight to Cairo.

I was told that there would be a four-hour stop over instead of two, due to some bad desert storm over the Arabian Peninsula.

Oh no! This was what I hated the most, waiting alone with nothing to do. I still called my husband out of sheer habit, and informed him of the delay of the flight to Cairo. It would take me quite some time getting used to the fact that we were separated.

My self-esteem had taken a beating and I was hurting deeply inside.

Having done the customary round of walking through the duty free shopping zone, I deliberated on a body massage vis a vis a foot massage. The latter won the day and after a relaxing foot therapy and a fresh coat of nail paint, I was ready to conquer the world.

Having run out of what more to do besides window-shopping, I picked up my de rigueur copy of the latest *Hello* magazine and walked back to the departure gate of my flight. Settling comfortably in a lounger, I was soon immersed in the latest international gossips and trends. However, even that failed to hold my interest after some time, and I looked up over my magazine, and almost froze.

Sitting right across me was my nemesis, deeply engrossed in some book. I slyly looked to see the author,

Albert Camus! Oh my, not only arrogant but also an intellectual snob to boot.

Just then he looked up and saw me staring at him and quirked his left eyebrow, as if saying, you again? And I sank behind the folds of my magazine with my heart beating, as if I was a teenager with raring hormones gone awry.

Why were the fates conspiring? Why did I keep on being in this stranger's path or should I say he on mine! I thought I had seen the last of him in Dubai and here he was on the same flight to Cairo and also aware of my destination.

The Emirates flight departure to Cairo broke my uneasy mood and I was all set for the final destination, secretly relieved to be seeing the last of that enigmatic snob, who for some reason had rubbed me on the wrong side.

The three and half-hour flight was uneventful and it was almost late evening when I arrived at the swanky Cairo International Airport.

After completing arrival formalities, I walked towards the baggage carousel and stood waiting for my bags, which seemed to be taking forever. After a delay of almost twenty minutes, I started to get a little anxious. I remembered an incident some years back, when my husband's two suitcases had been misplaced on arrival at Chicago.

It had been early winter and he had to undergo the inconvenience of buying new clothes and shoes.

He almost froze in the process because he had been wearing only a tee shirt and trousers when he had left Delhi.

I almost hyperventilated thinking about my treasured clothes and footwear lying lost and forlorn at some airport baggage section. Just then, I saw the distinct red of one of my suitcases. I heaved a visible sigh of relief and edged closer to the belt to lift off the bulky bag. In my nervous anticipation, as I struggled to remove the bag, just then a pair of arms bent across and effortlessly picked it off the belt and placed it near my feet.

My volley of profuse thanks got stuck in my throat when I saw that it was the same stranger, whom *Kismet* for some reason seemed to be throwing at me time and again.

Before I could say anything more, I saw him turn and pick his bag from the belt and walk off. Rather than feeling thankful for his gesture, I felt a little deflated and irritated at the way he had just ignored my thanks and walked off.

By then my second bag had also come and wheeling both my bags, I walked towards the arrival hall. I anxiously looked amongst the many chauffeurs for a placard bearing my name, finding none; I tried calling the tour operator. He was to send the car, which would be taking me to the Hotel Kempinski Nile, Cairo, which was going to be my luxurious abode for the next fortnight.

The flight delay, bad connectivity of the cell phone provider and the late night, was slowly getting me anxious. Normally I would have been with my husband who would have taken care of all these glitches, but here I was, on my solo self-discovery trip in a new country.

After umpteen attempts, I finally got across to the cab driver. He was being deliberately obtuse or did not seem to understand why I had been considerably delayed, and my futile efforts to get him to come back seemed to be wasted.

"Why is it that I have the misfortune of having to rescue you?" I angrily whirled around; now sufficiently aware it was my nemesis again. Why did he make me feel and look like a fumbling idiot, incapable of any decisions.

I politely enquired whether he had heard me asking for any assistance from him? If no, then should he not be on his way, and leave me to sort out my issues.

He shrugged and told me that I was welcome to do what I liked. He was merely being helpful to a fellow compatriot, and a woman who had clearly written all over her face that she was a tourist and to boot it, bordering on hysterical. For a few minutes I was dumbstruck with rage and had he been a little closer, I swear, I would have slapped his arrogant face!

Blindly I wheeled my suitcases and stepped out of the airport and went to the taxi counter from where I could take a taxi to the hotel. There was a very long queue, apparently caused by a labor strike.
I was quiet amused, this seemed like my own country! At the same time I was getting worried at the lateness of the hour and arrangements to reach the hotel.

Suddenly a car with the hotel logo stopped on the side. It was my sarcastic knight in shining armor! He told me to get into the car and not create any scene, as both of us were heading towards the same hotel.

"Much as I would like to leave you to your feminist ideas of independence, and I know that you don't need any man's help to get your problems sorted, I wish to sleep peacefully after a long and tiring flight. Without wondering whether that attractive Indian woman managed to reach her hotel or was wandering around like a lost sheep."

Before I could hurl back any retort to his insults and the one solitary compliment, he thrust his visiting card at me and said acidly, "My credentials, to put you at ease!"

My first instinct had been to throw his card back at him. I turned around and I saw the never- ending queue for the few taxis and realized the lateness of the hour. I was alone in a foreign country for the first time, and knew no one. At least, his had been the only consistent face that I had seen since Delhi.

So however much that irritated me, I swallowed my pride and I decided to jump in into the lion's pit. My eyes skimmed over the card, noting his name as Samarthya Singh. He was the Bureau Head of a reputed international news agency representing the Middle East and India.

Noting my look of relief, he almost sneeringly remarked, "What did you think I was, a street loafer on a look out for gullible women?"

I ignored his jibe and asked him how did he know which hotel I was staying?

He snickered, "I did not have to be Sherlock Holmes! Madam, you were loud enough to be heard in the nether world, when you were talking to your tour operator."

I looked down with embarrassment, feeling the hot course of blood pounding in my veins.

Sheepishly I got in to the luxurious hotel car and curled up as close to the window as I could. I saw him look at me with amusement and for once, I did not care and stared back at him. I had an attitude of "I-care-a-damn", and to my indignation he raised one quirky eyebrow as if saying he was impressed with my bravado.

The taxi sped thru Cairo. At another time I would have been excitedly soaking in the sights and sounds of a new city. However, the very thought of being in such a close confine with him was unnerving. It did not help that he was busy tapping away on his android, as if totally unaware of my presence. Well, two could play this game. I ignored him equally and looked out unseeingly from the window.

The chill in the taxi was enough to freeze a lake in summer!

After what seemed like an interminable time, we were at the hotel. Clambering out and mumbling my grateful thanks, which were received by S (I had decided to call him that, S suited him to the tee, S for sarcastic snob) with an amused smile. I quickly followed the porter to the reception for my check in formalities. I wanted to be as far away from S as was possible. Thankfully my luck held good for there were no glitches with my hotel bookings, which had been arranged through our family's travel house business.

Tired, emotionally and physically, I hit the bed as soon as I changed over in my demure nightwear, barely noticing the luxurious surroundings of my room.

Warm rays of the sun falling on my face woke me up and for a few minutes I was disoriented about my whereabouts!

I sat up on the bed elated, remembering my adventure and the stranger, who for some reason had been a part of it till now.

There was a feeling of excitement coupled with fear. For the first time in my life there was no one with me, telling me what I should be doing and I was reveling in this feeling of liberation!

I made myself a cup of tea and sent a text message to my sons about my safe arrival. I told them I would speak to them later in the evening. My husband had sent me a message checking with me if all was fine at my end and out of pure habit I texted back, letting him know about my day's plan.

I mentally chided myself to learn to be emotionally independent now, because I seriously did not know where my life would be going from this point of time. Would I always be taking the steps to resolve the stalemate that our marriage of twenty-two years was heading towards or would he, my husband, also meet me half way?

Shaking myself out of these feelings of pain and dejection, I went in for a quick but rejuvenating aroma bath. I mentally promised myself that while in Egypt, I would not think of the mess that my life was. I would immerse myself in this very first experience of freedom, however small it may be.

I had chalked out the plan for the day. Being a total history aficionado, I had planned to visit the Egyptian museum of antiquities at Tahrir Square as my first port of call. Keeping in mind my solitary status and the cultural sensibilities of the country, I wore loose white linen pants with a striped tee shirt and liberally used the sunscreen lotion on my skin.

I planned to walk the twenty minutes or so distance to the museum, hoping to immerse in the Cairo ethos.

I was hungry, as last night I had just crashed to bed without any dinner, and walked in to the hotel restaurant for the much-needed sustenance for my body.

My fantastic luck was holding up. The first person I see was Mr. High and Mighty Singh, and we both simultaneously walked in to the restaurant.

He was wearing a well-cut dark business suit, with a pristine white shirt and a floral red paisley tie. He looked more like a successful corporate top honcho, than some one from the media world.

He nodded to me, and I sourly thought, he expects a courtesy from me, with me bowing down to his majesty for according me such honors. I gave him my best frigid how-nice- to-see-you smile and turned to go in to the restaurant. It was almost ten and the place was full of tourists and just about every table was occupied.

The hostess on seeing Samarthya, greeted him effusively by name telling him how good it was to see him back after a long time, and immediately offered to take him to the last unoccupied table. She turned to me and apologized for the unusual rush and asked me to wait in the lounge for some time and that she would come and inform me as soon as a table was available.

I turned to go out when I heard Samarthya tell the hostess, "Maliha, don't bother, Madam will share the table with me," and then turning towards me said, "Don't you think you know enough of me, to be able to share the breakfast table? You are absolutely safe!" His eyes sweeping the wide room packed with people from different parts of the world.

Walking out would have made me look like a gauche school- girl and rather than giving him another opportunity in making me look churlish, I accepted his invite.

After loading my breakfast plate I came and sat at the table overlooking the scenic poolside.

"Good to see a woman with a healthy appetite."

Some how his remark irritated me as if implying I was a glutton.

"Since we seem fated to meet each other, let me reintroduce myself formally! I am Samarthya Singh from Delhi and I am working with MNS Broadcasting Corporation."

I was zapped to see sour face smiling and as if wonders never ceased, he was extending his hand in a friendly handshake. The moment I placed my hand in his, an electric current coursed through me. I nervously looked down hoping he had not noticed my reaction. I took a grip on my emotions and wondered what was wrong with me.

I was a mature woman about town! And here I was, struggling to concentrate on what he was saying. I did understand that he was there to cover a crucial Middle-East summit and some other assignment.

He smiled as he told me that he would be in Cairo for almost a fortnight. After the preliminary introductions, he asked what had brought me to Egypt.

I was reluctant to talk much and merely said that I was on a holiday for a fortnight and hoped to see Egypt as much as I could.

If he was curious about my being alone, he did not show it, and for that I was some how impressed with him. Most men would have been inquisitive about a single woman travelling alone, especially if she happened to be reasonably presentable.

I was pleasantly surprised when Samarthya offered advice regarding the places I could visit and also of the do's and don'ts that I had already apprised myself of. With that surreal feeling of truce, we took each other's leave.

I was bemused with this unexpected encounter with him and left the hotel with my GPS navigator on the phone guiding me to the best route to the museum.

The Museum of Antiquities transported me back to the age of the Pharaohs.

The ancient civilization had fascinated me right from my teenage years and here I was standing in front of the amazingly beautiful gold facemask of King Tutankhamun.

Hours passed in rapt attention, studying the treasures of the boy king and the tombs of Rameses III and Thutmosis III.

The section on Akhenaten and his famous queen Nefertiti, who abandoned the traditional Egyptian polytheism and worshipped one god –Aten the sun god- was very interesting.

The historical artifacts, which I had only read about so far, were being viewed by me with great pleasure. It was as if my dream had come true!

After a quick bite at the museum cafeteria, I was drawn to the ancient jewelry section.

Princess Neferuptah's neck collar made of gold, carnelian and feldspar beads had me wishing that I too were an Egyptian princess, of the middle period.

I would be decked up with kohl in my eyes and with the drop- dead collar around my neck. Well since the real one was out of reach, I bought a beautiful imitation of the same from the souvenir shop.

All good things come to an end and after a tiringly satisfying day, I took a taxi back to the hotel.

CHAPTER 2

$\mathbf{B}$ack in the cool confines of my room, I stripped off my clothes. I ran the bath with warm water liberally sprinkling it with some soothing bath salts and immersed my self in the bathtub to ease my now groaning muscles.

The strident ringing of the phone jolted me out of the languid stupor that I had slipped into, and I hurriedly reached for the telephone extension next to the bathtub.

I was wondering who could be calling me because I had already spoken to my sons and had texted my husband.

"Hi Serena, I am going to the Cairo Jazz Club for dinner, would you like to join me? You will enjoy it, it's quite an experience."

By now, I had come to recognize this cool drawling voice; it was Samarthya Singh on the other side of the line. For a few seconds I sat there amazed at this sudden invite.

He was being very hospitable after his arrogant behavior and I thought why not! I definitely would not be venturing out at night to a club on my own.

"Sure," I mumbled, too dumbstruck to actually analyze why I had agreed so readily to go out with him.

"I will meet you at the hotel lobby at 9 pm." The click of the phone being disconnected, made me realize I was still holding on to the receiver with a look of disbelief in my eyes.

I wondered what he would think of my easy acceptance of his offer and perhaps misconstrue that I was interested in him. Feeling a little stupid, I decided to give an excuse and opt out. Then I realized I did not know his room number and rather than calling the reception to connect to his room, I decided to go along with the invite.

Some how I knew he would know the reason for my refusal. I did not want to give him the pleasure of thinking that I was some dumb woman, who was eager for his company just because he was a handsome and enigmatic man. He must be aware that he made women go all weak-kneed and woolly -headed in his company.

So deciding to behave like a sophisticated woman who is comfortable going out with a man she barely knows, I got down to getting ready for the outing.

Quickly finishing with my bath, I spent some feverish minutes contemplating the most difficult task we women face, deciding what to wear!

I settled on a midnight blue silk sheath dress, which I had added at the last minute and was now glad at having done so. I had brought no suitable jewelry and so I decided to wear the neck collar I had bought at the museum.

Standing in front of the mirror I was glad I did so, because it looked fabulous and I felt like a queen! With quick deft strokes, I applied a light makeup and dabbed my favorite Paloma Picasso perfume.

I realized that it was already quarter to nine and quickly slipped on my strappy-heeled designer sandals. With my Prada evening bag gracing my hand, I was ready to face Samarthya Singh on equal terms as a cool sophisticate.

Coming down the lift, I hurriedly gave a lookover in the elevator mirror and was again assailed by feelings of doubt. Was I doing the right thing, going out on a dinner date with an almost stranger? Stepping out of the elevator and feeling a little unsettled, I looked around the hotel lobby for Samarthya.

"I am impressed, a woman who is on time! I thought I would have to cool my heels waiting for you," came the laconic drawl from somewhere behind me.

I turned around to see Samarthya wearing a well-tailored black suit, teemed with a black silk shirt open at the neck. For a few moments I was speechless, he was looking amazingly handsome, his salt and pepper hair curling around the neck of his black shirt giving him a rakish air. I could almost hear my heart pounding away and felt a rush of blood suffuse my face. Oh God, I hope he could not see me blushing like some simpleton out on her first date.

Gathering my wits, I acidly retorted that this was just a simple dinner outing, indirectly implying that it did not merit any special efforts.

"Your exotic neck piece belies your answer. You are looking good." With one swift retort, he contradicted and complimented me, leaving me annoyed and at the same time smug with womanly vanity.

S was self- driving a black Audi and helped me to the passenger seat. I was secretly impressed with his chivalrous courtesy, which many a men in our modern times seem to overlook.

S told me that the Cairo Jazz Club was a popular nightspot for the rich Egyptians and expats. The key attraction was the stage, which saw local and international artists entertain the crowds with musical performances. Having a very eclectic taste in music, I started looking forward to my night out, hoping to hear some local bands play on the stage.

The atmosphere in the car was for some reason very companionable, both of us comfortably lost in our thoughts and I was happy letting the magic of nighttime Cairo grip me.

My eyes were eagerly soaking in the sights and also surreptitiously watching my companion and wondering about this other side of his personality.

He had appeared downright rude from the very first moment I had set sights on him, but at the same time I had to grudgingly admit that he had helped me in all my predicaments.

S turned at that very moment when I was intently watching him and with a small laugh asked if he had passed the test!

I seemed to be making a habit of blushing, which was so silly considering I was a mature woman in her forties, and was glad of the darkness in the car.

S realizing my embarrassment diverted the topic and started telling me that we were crossing the Nile on the 15 May Bridge and would be at the club in Darb Al Agoza in a short while.

At that moment I grudgingly acknowledged in my mind that he was a gentleman, being glad that I had given in to my impulsive affirmative to S to go out for dinner with him.

The Jazz club was an amazing experience. The predominantly orangish brown walls and the ceiling lit with colored glass lights gave the club a very exotic vibrant look. The crowd was multicultural and it was quite a change to see the local Egyptian women in a different avatar from what one would see on the streets.

I was fortunate because it happened to be the day when one of Cairo's famous live bands, "Wust El Balad" was playing. The dim lights and the thumping music from the speakers had the crowd swaying to the funky music, which was a blend of traditional Arab and western music.

My love for music and the infectious beat could not keep me away from the dance floor. It was another matter that I was blessed with two left feet but what the hell, I was so caught up in that electric atmosphere that I asked S to come and join me on the floor, as if I had known him for ever and it was the most natural thing to do!

S laughed and joined me, professing that he could not dance to save his skin, unless of course he had downed some shots of vodka to give him the Dutch courage. I waived his excuse off saying that we both sailed in the same boat. The next hour had us shuffling and grinding away on the crowded dance floor. I don't know what dance moves we were doing, but I was enjoying myself immensely!

After a long time I had let myself go and that too with a person I hardly knew. Sometimes I think it is the easiest to do that, of letting your defenses down with a stranger, because he is not going to be judging you and even if he does, would it matter?

S finally pleaded exhaustion and I laughingly let him pull me away to the dinner table. The time had passed so quickly and I realized it was close to midnight.

We ordered a bottle of Egypt's most rich and elegant wine "Chateau des Reves" made from a variety of grapes imported from Lebanon.

Dinner was an exotic affair with Samarthya ordering a stuffed chicken breast with Mozzarella and Pesto. I settled for a chicken Messakhan, a half chicken, laid over roasted pita bread served with garlic yoghurt.

The food was delicious and the next half hour or more passed in pleasant comfort enjoying the meal.

I looked up at one instance and saw S watching me, with an intent look that was disconcerting. I quickly turned away pretending to watch the people on the dance floor. I did not even want to analyze it, let alone question him.

It was almost two in the night by the time we left. The wine, food and the dancing all coupled together, made me pleasantly drowsy and it had been an effort to keep myself awake during the ride back to the hotel.

When we reached the hotel, S had his right arm around my shoulders. It was not as if I was drunk, more like I was sleep walking and despite my protestations he walked me to my room.

At the door, while I was fumbling to remove the key card from my evening bag, S took the bag and retrieving the card swiped open the door.

I turned to thank him for the lovely evening almost tripping on my heels and S reached out to hold me in his arms.

I felt as if a thousand volts of electricity had hit me, with the warmth of his body seeping into me.

For a few seconds time stood still, and breaking out of the tense reverie, I almost stuttered, thanking him for the wonderful evening.

All the easy camaraderie of the earlier evening at the club seemed to have gone somewhere and the present seemed fraught with an unsaid tension. S smiled and after bidding me a good night, left me standing at my room door. Why did my words sound so phony to me, did they seem so to S too?

All sleep seemed to have eluded me; I was wide-awake thinking about the evening that had gone by. I stood in front of the bathroom mirror looking at a reasonably attractive woman in her mid forties.

What was happening to me? What was this untenable attraction that I was feeling towards S? I barely knew him other than where he worked. Was I so vulnerable at this point of life that any stranger could affect me in such a manner? At the Club, our conversation had been very general and both of us had, as if, avoided talking about our personal lives.

With these strange feelings clouding my mind, I lay on the bed. Sleep was miles away and much as I tried not to think about S, the mind veered towards him, and for one forbidden moment, I wondered, what it would be like, to be held in his arms and kissed passionately. The thought in it self was so sensual! I would probably melt in his arms if he actually even touched me!

I shook myself mentally and scolded my self for harboring such scandalous thoughts, and sternly told myself to keep away from that path and curb my fantasies.

Deep down, I knew I was trying to overcome the rejection that I was facing as a woman. A woman who knew she was of some worth, and a loving and passionate woman to top that.

It was almost early morning when I finally let sleep ensnare me and it was the ringing of my cellphone that awoke me. For a few moments I was wondering where I was. Blindly, I reached for the phone and realized it was a call from my son. I was instantly awake and glad to hear from him. We chatted for some time and I told him what I had seen and done but for some reason did not talk about my last night's rendezvous.

I was not ready to share it, knowing deep down that I had not done the right thing.

Finally I got ready and came down around ten, just in time for a late breakfast. Not very hungry, I just ate some fresh fruits and finished breakfast with a cup of tea. I was not much of a tea or coffee drinker, and unlike many, I could start my day without any special need for it. However the late last night had taken it's toll and I needed the zing to take the day head on!

My second day in Cairo was going to be exciting! Ever the eternal shopaholic, I had decided to go to the

Khan el Khalili souk. This has been in existence since the 14 th century and was still equally vibrant and lively. No visit to Cairo can be complete without having walked the charming narrow labyrinth of alleys that abound the souk.

The next few hours were the most exciting times I had, my senses bombarded with the countless shops selling just about anything. You name it, from spices to silver jewelry, souvenirs, carpets, and I simply fell in love with the Egyptian glass lanterns.

I had been forewarned to haggle without any shame and spent time bargaining with good humor. I finally walked away, the proud owner of a pair of beautifully colored glass lanterns, which I would have probably got for twice the price in a fancy mall.

Wiki travels had recommended the Fishawi's Ahwa as one of Cairo's oldest cafes in the El Khalili souk for a cup of strongly brewed tea or smoke the many fruit flavored shisha.

I settled for an "Ahwa Ariha" (coffee lightly sweetened) and sat back with complete leisure enjoying the hustle and bustle of the world pass me by.

Time stood still for me; I was lost in an exotic world! Here I was a woman, all alone, enjoying her newfound independence. Never in a zillion years, I would have envisaged my self in such a situation and I was thoroughly enjoying myself.

For those moments, I let my mind block the upheaval that had turned my life upside down.

Back at the hotel, I deliberated over going down for dinner or ordering in the room. The former won, as I wanted to try the food at the restaurant, which served excellent Ottoman dishes.

I wanted to fully experience my new found courage and what better than walking in solo at a fancy restaurant without the de rigueur male companion. Dressing simply in beige linen pants and an off white silk shirt, I was shown by the maître d' to a corner table.

After settling in, I had this strange sensation, and looked up and saw Samarthya directly across my table. He was deep in conversation with an attractive woman. She seemed to be an Egyptian in her early thirties with streaked blonde hair and an extremely attractive face, and I uncharitably thought, colored hair of course! Her ruby red dress was clinging at all the right places and she was oozing with oomph. She was talking animatedly with Samarthya and looked, as if she would probably devour him with her eyes if she could. I felt a wave of searing jealousy course through me, when I saw her place her hands on his.

At that moment, I wanted to snatch her hand off and tell her to get lost! Just then Samarthya looked up and I found myself staring right in to his eyes. I was so embarrassed to be caught staring at them, and even though he acknowledged me by giving me a smile and dipping his head, I felt like a thief who had been caught and just looked down.

Fortunately for me, the maître d' came in just then and asked me about my drink preference.

All my pleasure seemed to have evaporated. Why was I so perturbed at seeing him with another woman? I had no claims on him or his time, then why this feeling of betrayal and jealousy. The excellent food and service did nothing to alleviate my mood. My eyes, much against my will, would surreptitiously be drawn to the opposite table. Somehow the meal got over and I took great pains to make sure that I did not pass by Samarthya's table.

Coming back to my room, I changed and got into my bed. I was still feeling restless and I switched on the television and mindlessly watched Julia Roberts romancing Hugh Grant in Notting Hill.

At another time I would have watched this movie with as much interest as watching it for the first time. I was being stupid; I was letting a mere passing attraction for a handsome stranger rule my life. There was no such thing as attraction at first sight because I definitely will not use the clichéd love at first sight statement. Anyways I was done with loving.

Just then the intercom buzzed and I absently picked up the phone and almost dropped it on hearing Samarthya's voice on the other side. "Serena, sorry calling you late once again. I seem to be making it a habit once too often. I have a day off tomorrow and wanted to know what you were planning to do?"

I was very surprised to hear this from him, reluctantly telling him that I was planning to go see the Sphinx and the pyramids.

"Great! Then I can take you and I will also get to play the tourist. Is it not surprising that I have visited Cairo so often but have yet to see them? The other day I seem to have been caught by your infectious interest in the Egyptian history! So do you think you can be ready by seven in the morning? I know it's rather early but then the later we leave, the hotter it will get."

I was amazed at his audacity, calling me late in the night and then without any preamble, deciding that I would be going with him. What made him think that I was dying for his company and would, at the drop of a hat, go with him just because he had decided to grace me with his company!

Before I could give some excuse for not going with him, He laughed and said, "Don't try to give any excuses because I know you are going to come up with some lame one. Are you going to slink away quietly like you did in the restaurant, and act as if you did not know me, when I had looked at and acknowledged you!"

Thank God for the phone line, because I was blushing furiously with embarrassment. He was the same person with whom I had spent a fabulous late evening yesterday. I had for some reason been downright rude to him in the restaurant and deep down I knew the reason for the same and was not willing to acknowledge it.

I had been jealous to see Samarthya with another woman! How was that possible? In such a short span of time how could he affect me so? It was the state of my mental being; I was feeling vulnerable and was clutching at straws in vain.

"Hello, where are you? So it's decided we are going together."

I could not but agree, after having behaved so immaturely in the evening. Also deep in my heart I wanted to know this enigmatic stranger. For some reason the maturity befitting my age always seemed to desert me where he was concerned. Was I in the throes of experiencing what was called a holiday romance? Or maybe I needed to bolster my womanly ego and pride and what better way than basking in the attentions of an attractive man!

CHAPTER 3

Early morning saw me dressed in white linen palazzos and a paisley print muslin long sleeves shirt. I also loosely knotted a jewel- toned scarf around my neck, to avoid the ravages of the sun, which was not kind to the skin, especially, when one hits the forties. I wore my favourite purple sneakers, because I knew there would be a fair amount of walking to be done. Donning my Tiffany aviator glasses, I picked up my bag and a wide brimmed straw hat and walked down to the hotel lobby.

I could see Samarthya deep in conversation with the hotel concierge and was glad because it gave me the momentary respite I needed every time I saw this attractive man. Just at that moment he looked up and gave me a wave and I was glad of my dark aviators that hid the star struck look in my eyes.

"Good morning Serena, you seem to be amongst the rare breed of women who is punctual. Let's leave; we can have breakfast at Giza because we must avoid the rush hour of Cairo."

We drove out of Cairo beating the maddening traffic and were soon driving southward towards Giza. Samarthya, who had donned a dark pair of aviators, was looking absolutely handsome in a very dark sensual way.

When he smiled at me and asked me if I was enjoying the drive and my holiday, I almost stuttered my reply. God, this was bordering on ridiculous and I seemed like a stuck up record, which did not go beyond seeing how crazily attractive this man was! I was surely and absolutely falling in love or should I say, in lust with him.

My holiday had taken off on another dimension! A forbidden and an exciting one, which I knew, I should not be embarking on. I was like a moth drawn to the fire knowing that I would be singed, but had become reckless and did not seem to care. I wanted to live in the moment and forget the reality of my life.

"Serena, we are almost there," S's voice shook me out of my forbidden thoughts.

At that moment I felt silly and angry with my self for my lack of control over my emotions.

I had come to Egypt to see the Great Pyramids of Giza. Here they were in front of my eyes and I was busy mooning over an almost stranger.

"You are amazing Serena," I chastised myself.

After parking the car, S and I first decided to have a quick breakfast before we started our long tour of the Giza Pyramids. In the café, Samarthya professed that in all his trips he had not visited the pyramids.

I laughingly shamed him for not seeing the oldest seven wonders of the ancient world, which were largely intact!

"History has not been one of my favorite subjects! And I don't particularly care about all these monuments," S replied.

Before I could hold myself back, I ended up asking him what had made him come today!

S looked at me enigmatically and with a smile replied, "The pleasure of being in the company of a woman who is not only beautiful but also intelligent and bold enough to know what she wants in life and to go for it."

For one moment my breath seemed to have been drawn out of me. I did not know how to respond to his cool and honest compliment.

Gathering my wits and making light of his remark, I told him that it was good for him that he had met me otherwise he would have missed seeing a wonder of the world. S merely smiled as we made our way to the Giza pyramids.

He had arranged for a tour guide and I was glad he had done that, because the Giza plateau was scattered with a number of pyramids.

Hussain our guide was very well versed with history and had a way, as most tour guides have, of making it doubly interesting. The complex had three pyramids, the Khufu, Khafre and Menkaure and of course the massive sculpture associated with Egypt – the Great Sphinx. It was tiring and dusty but immensely satisfying to see these massive man made structures made around two thousand five hundred years back.

The pyramid at Khufu is the largest pyramid ever built, it has 2.3 million stone blocks weighing an average of 2.5 tons to 15 tons each.

My excitement knew no bounds; here I was devouring these amazing structures with my eyes. At one time in life I had been so fascinated with Egyptology, that I had wanted to be an archaeologist working with the team of famous Egyptologist Zahi Hawass digging ancient Egyptian treasures.

But then all my dreams had remained dreams, always lost, living the expectations of others around me. Words came to my mind.

> **Like a buoy**
> **Unfixed and bobbing**
> **life spent chartering safe passages for**
> **others to live.**

Inside the Khufu pyramid, for one moment, I had felt claustrophobic in the narrow sloping passages. I had instinctively clutched S's arm and then with embarrassment released it as fast.

This time I stumbled and Samarthya firmly took hold of my hand and held it all through our tour of the pyramids, giving me a look that said, that before I fall and he has to rescue me again, he might as well hold it!

It had seemed so natural to be walking hand in hand amongst the pyramids, as if we were a couple. Some would have been surprised by our comfort in each other's company, if they had known that we had met just a couple of days back.

Whatever, I did not want to understand the meaning of all this and was just flowing along with the tide of emotions which were engulfing me.

S took a number of photographs of me next to the pyramids and the sphinx. There was as if an unsaid understanding, that we would not have a photo of us clicked together.

Hussain our guide at one point offered to click both of us and rather than refusing his offer and creating an odd situation, S posed along with me. He placed his arm on my shoulders and I gave him the look that said, it was not necessary, at which he just smiled wickedly holding me more closer to him.

The photo had come out very well, capturing Samarthya's quirky smile. I was smiling albeit a little stiff, because of his sexy presence right beside me. I had decided I would delete it from my digital camera but felt a twinge of regret in doing so and impulsively called Samarthya, asking him if he needed a copy of the photo.

"Have you decided to keep the photograph? I was under the impression that you would have it deleted at the first possible instance. And yes you can give me a copy of the same, I have no problems."

I wanted to retort back to him that since he did not know my situation, it was easy for him to say anything. How could I explain to my family that here was a man, I had barely met a couple of days back and here I was, standing pretty cozy with his arm on my shoulders. How would they react, if I told them that I was slowly burning with a maddening desire for him?

The long day came to an end, with both Samarthya and I enjoying a panoramic view of the pyramids and the Great Sphinx at sundown. That moment would always be frozen in my mind, as something bordering on the magical.

On the drive back we were both lost in our own thoughts. It seemed so natural that we did not need to converse. I felt so comfortable and relaxed, and it was with a start I realized that we had reached the hotel.

It was taken for granted that after a long day together, we would have dinner with each other. We decided to have it before going back to our respective rooms despite being bone tired.

Just yesterday night I had heartburns over S's dinner date, and here I was today with him in a corner table all to myself. It was another matter that I was behaving in a very nonchalant manner lest Mr. handsome could guess the tumultuous state of my mind.

Dinner was a quiet affair and I thanked S for the wonderful time I had had. He smiled saying that he had enjoyed exploring the pyramids and had been infected with my enthusiasm to explore Egypt.

Soon we were walking out of the restaurant, towards the lift lobby. S was on a floor above mine and as always, he courteously came along to see me off to my room.

After unlocking my room, I turned once again to thank him. S waived it off, saying he had enjoyed my company equally and maybe we could figure out some more sight seeing trips. He laughingly added that he really needed to catch up on the wonders of Egypt, before they disappeared.

My heart literally soared with pleasure on hearing this, and I probably must have given myself away by the slow flush coloring my cheeks.

It came as an electrifying shock to me when S lightly brushed my cheek. He smiled and raising his one brow with amusement said,

"You blush! You are such a refreshing change."

He turned and said he better go lest he got tempted to do some thing more.

I once again felt a rush of heat on my face and quickly turned and entered my room. Oh God, this was crazy, I was behaving as if I was a teenager in the throes of a new love. I told myself to take a grip on my emotions and enjoy S's company while I was here on my holiday.

It seemed so ridiculous I was blushing and cautioning my self, once too many times. I think I should have the honesty to say that I was attracted to Samarthya and I wanted to be with him, definitely during this holiday.

Why do we women have to be coy when expressing our needs and wants unlike most men who are ever willing to take a chance without any feelings of guilt or remorse?

CHAPTER 4

The ringing room phone at that time meant it had to be S, and with a beating heart, I picked up the receiver, unable to respond for a few moments.

S asked me if I was ok and I replied I was fine, merely tired after a long and fabulous day.

He told me that he was going for a day to Alexandria and would be back the day after tomorrow. He was thinking of taking a couple of days off from work and laughingly asked me if I would be interested in being his guide for all the things he should be seeing!

My heart almost skipped a beat with the anticipation of spending time with S and I was stupefied with the turn of events. I was struggling badly to overcome this maddening desire for this handsome man and wondered if there was some way I could avoid him and the ensuing heartbreak that was sure to follow.

"Does your silence mean that you don't want me as your travel partner?" and like a fool I cried out that I would love to have his company.

"Then let me be back and we will sit down and plan our travel trip, I don't want you blaming me for making you miss seeing your precious monuments."

I laughed and agreed that better not happen. We bid goodnight and for a long time I could not sleep. I was excited yet nervous about being in a prolonged contact with S and wondered what this would lead to.

The next day dawned, all bright and cheerful. Samarthya had left early morning for Alexandria. After having a leisurely breakfast, I decided to spend the first half by the poolside, reading and generally lounging around. I was still lethargic after yesterday's trip to the pyramids. While at the poolside, I got chatting with two American women from Los Angeles. They were going to visit the Hanging Church (El Muallaqa) in Coptic Cairo, a part of old Cairo, post lunch. Suzanne, one of the women, asked me if I wanted to come along and I readily agreed, as it would be more fun to have company while visiting a new place.

So post lunch we trouped off in a taxi that took us to the old part of Cairo. I thoroughly enjoyed the day visiting one of the oldest churches in Egypt, whose history dates back to almost the 3rd century AD.

We also visited the fascinating Coptic Museum occupying over 8000sq metres featuring almost 16000 objects of importance to the Copts of Egypt.

After thanking Suzanne and Annette for their company, I was back in my room pleasantly tired but happy that I was fully enjoying my trip to Egypt. I called my sons and chatted with them about the exciting time I was having, of course never mentioning my new attractive companion. I was ready for a warm and relaxing bath, having decided that I would opt for a room service. I did not feel like dressing up and going down. There was another reason too, at the back of my mind I knew S was not there.

The pleasure of being in his company was becoming something of a habit for me. This habit could only lead to heartbreak and pain.

It was almost nine thirty in the morning when I got up. I had slept deeply after many days as if some inner tension had eased in me.

I rose up, still lethargic and went about my bath like an automaton. I selected a sleeveless floral dress and tied my hair in a loose knot and slipped on my flat sandals and went down for my breakfast.

I decided to sit by the patio near the pool and just had cut fruits with a croissant and a cup of tea. S had said that he would be back in Cairo around midday. I was deliberating whether to wait for him or go about on my own. My predicament was solved; S called on my mobile saying that he was reaching the hotel in an hour's time.

I decided to go back to my room and wait for S. I lay on the bed listening to my favorite band, Passenger, crooning soft songs, which were like poems strung to music, on my iPod.

I must have dozed off because I got up on hearing the room bell buzzing insistently thru the headphones. I rushed to open the door lest who ever was on the other side thought of breaking it open next.

On opening the door I found it was Samarthya who looked very annoyed, he came inside the room asking me what the hell had I been doing?

He had called on my mobile and the room intercom many times and had got worried on getting no response and on top I had taken my own sweet time to open the door because of the headphones.

I looked sheepishly at him and told him I had dozed off with the headphones listening to the music.

"Oh God, Serena, you scared the hell out of me!" Saying this, S pulled me in his arms and started kissing me.

This was totally out of the blue; a bolt of lightening hit me. I did not even get a chance to escape. What had started as an angry punitive kiss slowly changed to a gentle exploration of my lips.

I don't know when my hands instead of pushing him away, locked themselves around his neck. We were fused to each other, lip to lip, his arms holding me tight against his chest and I was totally lost in this maelstrom of physical pleasure.

S let go of my lips and I gulped for some air, like a person drowning, gasping for a breath of air!

We looked at each other with intense emotions, unable to fathom what had happened at that instance. It seemed like our barrier of restraint had fallen apart. We had laid our selves open to the fact which both of us had been subconsciously denying, that we were attracted to each other.

"I am not going to say I am sorry about this! I have been wanting to kiss you from the very first time you fell in my arms!" said S.

I protested saying that I had not fallen in his arms and he was being very presumptuous about his sex appeal.

"Please, I am sorry, I don't know what came over me," I said to S and went and stood by the window, my face all flushed with the emotions I had experienced.

Samarthya came and stood behind me and kissed the nape of my neck and that just broke all my self-control and I turned melting in his arms.

I don't know how and when we fell on the bed, with S lying over me, his strong sinewy thighs holding my lower body captive. We were kissing each other deeply, our tongues entwined, exploring each other. His hands were feverishly tugging open the buttons of my blouse and then pushing aside my bra exposing my aroused breasts.

I almost reared up with sensual shock when his lips locked with one of the peaks and started sucking it.

It came as a shock to me when I realized that I was begging him to make love to me. The sound of moaning that I could hear was mine. I came to my senses, and with a rush of shame tried to push him away.

He immediately lifted his head with a question in his passion filled eyes.

"Please I am sorry, I don't know what came over me. I am sorry," I once again mumbled and pulled myself off the bed.

"Serena, I am not going to deny that I want you, though you may deny, your body tells me some thing else."

How could I tell him that I wanted him too, but cried out to him that it was not right, since we both were married. Would we not be cheating on our partners?

I stood near the window my hands trembling, trying to button my blouse and my mind shocked with my body's reaction. All this while my attraction towards S had been in the privacy of my mind. I think I had successfully kept it hidden there, but my traitorous body had betrayed me in a moment.

Samarthya now knew that I was as attracted to him physically, as he was. I would be a hypocrite if I denied these feelings.

"I am sorry Samarthya, I did not mean this to happen," I cried out to him.

"Please can you forget about this and can we continue being the friends we have enjoyed being till now. I will not deny that I immensely look forward to your company being deeply attracted to you. However my life is in a mess at this point and I am trying to sort out the mess."

I could not at that moment share the sad facts of my married life. In fact I was using that as a defense against the unreasonable attraction I felt towards him.

"I cannot and do not want any diversions, whether physical or emotional at this point of my life. I am once again sorry if I have some how given you the impression that I am looking for some holiday romance."

"It's perfectly fine Serena, you do not have to give any justifications for your actions. I have never forced myself on a woman or needed to do so ever in my life," was his lightly sarcastic reply.

I cried out that was not the case, I was to blame as much, probably more so, since I knew that I did not want to be on that plain of emotions.

"We have experienced how our bodies react to each other honestly, though your mind denies the same. Serena I am not going to deny that I am attracted to you and need you physically.

I have no qualms in admitting that I will keep on trying to get you."

"Also while you are here in Egypt, do not even think for a moment, that you can avoid my company. I am a stubborn man, getting what I want."

I was dumbstruck and a little scared by what Samarthya had just said. My heart was racing with a nervous tension and my mind trying to comprehend that S was attracted and determined to get me.

For a moment I felt a burst of womanly pride at being desired so fiercely. But in the next moment, got back to my gutsy fiery self and told S that he could wait till eternity.

He merely laughed, came and without any-if-I-may-please, took me in his arms. He cupped my face in his hands and bent down and kissed me hard on my lips. His tongue trying to force open my lips. I was caught unaware by this sudden sensual assault and I hit out on his chest with my hands. S merely grabbed them and held them behind my back.

"You arrogant bas…" before I could complete my swear word, S took control. His tongue snaking into my open mouth and exploring and teasing me to play the mating game. I tried to bite him in anger and he almost tilted my head down by pulling my hair.

I cried out in pain and S ground out saying, "Stop being the vixen then!"

I was almost breathless and my groan of pleading got through to him and as suddenly, he let go of me. I would have fallen had it not been for my hands reaching out to hold him.

Samarthya pulled me in to his arms crying out, "Oh Serena, you are driving me crazy but I will respect your wishes and do nothing, till you want it."

"Let us meet in some time over an early dinner and discuss our trip to the temples of Abu Simbel."

I was wondering how this stranger who I did not know till a few days back had taken control of my life and felt a little annoyed by his presumptuousness in deciding how and where I should be going on my holiday!

"Samarthya, please do not stretch your schedules for me, I can go to Abu Simbel myself. I would have gone myself, had I not met you," I said to him with a small laugh.

"Yes you would have! But that was before we met, so let's not get into that discussion," Saying this S walked out of the room. He turned to remind me to be ready and meet him in the lobby.

In half hour's time I went down wearing my pair of blue denims and a tee and my hair scrunched up in a tight bun, looking as plain and dowdy as I could.

Let S see that I was a middle aged woman who was not always dressed up twenty four seven. I was a plain Jane and he would have to accept me in all my avatars.

I looked around the lobby and found him sitting in a corner sofa, engrossed doing something on his ipad. He looked up and smiled and gestured to me to sit besides him. He wanted a few more minutes as he was figuring out our travel schedule to Abu Simbel, which we would discuss over dinner.

I sat besides S, watching him; he was a handsome specimen of the male species. His dark hair liberally sprinkled with silver added to his stature. His strong angular jaw with a cleft gave him a rakish and sensual look. I was most fascinated with his hooded mysterious eyes that seemed to look down in to my very soul.

While I was dreamily looking on to him, he winked and gave me a deadly smile and asked me whether I was happy with what I was seeing or did I want something more.

For once, I did not blush and gave Mr. Smarty pants a fitting retort.

"Yes you will do, a few alterations here and there and you should be good! In fact more than good," and gave him a wide teasing smile.

But then he always had to have an upper hand. He bent over and frazzled my nerves with a sweet sensual kiss, holding my head with one hand lest I moved away. Only when he felt his exploration of my lips was complete did the wicked man let me go.

As always he had this knack of getting under my skin. He then got up and holding me by my hand walked with me to the restaurant. We seemed like a married couple and for one moment I wished, I had taken the pains to dress up and match up to this handsome man. But I had this womanly smugness that said how- ever dowdy or plain I may be looking, I was the woman who was walking besides him. I was the woman he wanted to make love to and not the many beautiful women who were giving him the come hither looks.

We sat in a secluded corner table and S outlined our three day trip to Aswan while we waited for our dinner to be served.

He checked with me whether he had left out any monument or places that I wished to see.

All this while I was listening and thinking how easy it was to fall in agreement with this good looking man. He was arrogant most of the time, yet showed you glimpses of his personality that made you want him for some thing more than a holiday romance.

Shaking myself from this fanciful dream, I tackled my dinner with an enjoyment that had S chuckle and say that I was a woman who was not counting the calories.

He gave me a thoroughly wicked look, saying not that it showed but maybe I could do with losing a few pounds.

My fluctuating weight was an issue that I had been fighting a battle with, ever since I had hit an early menopause. On hearing S tease me, I bantered with him that he should find a slimmer friend and to stop making fun of me, lest I swung a heavy hand towards him.

Samarthya ducked playfully and said, "Serena I like the way you look and truthfully any more or any less, it's not going to be you."

I was flattered; a slow flush of pleasure showed on my face and S gently touched my cheeks and then started kissing my hand. It seemed like my hand had no will, it just lay there limply subjecting itself to a sensual torture.

He was dropping light kisses on each finger and I was like a terrified animal that is in the sight of the predator, unable to move and save it's life. When S raised my hand

and took my index finger in his mouth to gently suck it, I broke out of this trance and pulled my hand away, frantically looking around to see if anyone had noticed this blatant display of carnal play. He laughed, understanding my agitation and wickedly said,

"This secluded table selection had been a calculated one."

The mood on the table suddenly changed from light-hearted bantering to one of simmering sexual tension.

We were done with dinner and I was eager to get away from the scene and said no to a selection of desserts being offered.

I wanted to have a cup of strong tea after the emotionally exhausting day, and the present scenario was also not helping.

When Samarthya said that he would like a cup of strong tea, and asked me if I would like to go to a teahouse that he frequented, I wanted to say no.

But somehow I could not deny myself his company that I craved deep in my heart. I was the moth drawn to the candle flame, dead sure that I was going to be singed badly, but some how the light was too attractive for me to ignore and I was recklessly heading towards doom.

We walked out of the restaurant, S holding me by my waist as if it was the most natural thing for him to do. I should have been resenting this, but was some how relishing the feeling of womanly pride of being able to attract such a handsome man.

Samarthya as always helped me in the passenger seat, which I found so chivalrous. My husband had never pampered me with such courtesies, except during our courting days.

I wonder if men do this only when they are out to attract and get a woman?

The earlier sexual tension was now missing in the car. S, like a master magician sensing my state of mind had selected some soothing tape of Zen music.

The half hour drive got us to this teahouse overlooking the Nile. It was a beautiful full moon night and the pleasant weather was just right for the sit-out overlooking the Nile. We sat there in a companionable comfort, sipping our teas, not feeling any need to speak.

It came as a major surprise, when Samarthya started telling me about his self.

CHAPTER 5

"I was born in a village off the beaten track in the Chamba valley of Himachal Pradesh. My father Devi Singhji was a schoolteacher. He was passionate about seeking knowledge and imparting the same to the village children, who were practically cut off from the rest of the world. He would spin stories about faraway places, telling about people living in far-flung corners of the world and happenings that were changing the world.

This was probably the only time my father could hold my total attention, for I was the prankster of the village and nothing could hold my attention for long. It was my father's passion that subconsciously gave a birth to this career that I am in today.

My mother Tara Devi was a gentle homemaker whose life revolved around her husband and myself, her only progeny."

"Life was making ends meet on a school teacher's salary with my mother pitching in by making jams and preserves which she sold to a local cooperative." I sat enraptured listening to Samarthya's deep timbered voice take me through a kaleidoscope of his childhood memories.

I felt transported back in time, reliving the number of moments S had got in to some foolhardy escapades and the number of heartburns he gave to his mother.

I laughed with him, feeling the same amount of unholy glee when they had locked the village dog in the temple with many tin cans tied to his tail. The pitiful howls and the cacophony of sounds had almost the whole village up in the night. The priest hyperventilating about the sacredness of the temple being desecrated, had earned S a sound thrashing from his father.

I also agreed that he deserved the thrashing more for terrorizing the dog than upsetting the priest, for I have a soft heart where animals are concerned.

I understood the pain he felt on losing his pet dog Sheru to a mountain bear. It seemed so unbelievable that this mature and capable man had been a child, giving in to all the foibles of childhood.

Samarthya's life took a tragic turn when he turned fifteen. He lost his father to an unexpected flash flood, which hit their village one night after a cloud burst in the upper reaches of the mountain valley. His father was swept away right in front of his eyes after helping him and his mother reach safer grounds.

Overnight from a precocious naughty boy, S became a serious young man. His mother bore the loss of her husband stoically, shutting herself in her own world. She immersed herself day and night working, and the decent insurance money that was paid to her, ensured that S did not miss out anything in his life. The only thing that brought her out of her shell was her almost obsessive concern about him pursuing his higher studies.

Samarthya travelled daily almost two hours one way to reach the senior school in the district, having promised himself that he would fulfill his father's dream of getting a good education and seeing the world that Master Devi Singhji had seen only in the pages of books.

Time just flew and in no time, Samarthya, having done extremely well, got an admission in a reputed college in Delhi. His mother sold off a little piece of land that she had been holding on to, just for this day.

"I threw myself in to studies, never having the time nor the luxury like the rich boys from the city to enjoy life. During my post graduation years, I used to work part time in the evenings in a coaching school, helping students prepare for the civil services. By now I was clear, that I was going to seek a career in the field of mass communication."

"I topped my class ensuring that I was the first among the many, to be selected for a job as a field reporter in a reputed news agency."

"My new career took me all over India, my forte being political news and I started living my father's dream. My thirst for knowledge led me to pursue additional courses equipping me to better my prospects in life. I tried getting my mother to leave the peaceful environs of the village to be with me, but it was a futile exercise. She was a hill woman and moreover my father's memories still tied her to the place."

"I ensured that she did not lack any physical comforts in life, though till her death a couple of years back, she kept on making jams and preserves for the local cooperative, enlisting the help of few young girls from the village.

She was a tough and independent woman and I miss her".

I gently placed my hand on Samarthya's, offering comfort for a loss that I could empathize with, having lost my own mother a few months back.

"So how and when did you meet your wife?" This was a question that had been burning on the tip of my tongue for a long time.

It was almost 12 in the night when S looked at his watch and patting my cheek gently said, "this is all for now, habibti, you need your beauty sleep. We will talk about that some other day soon."

I wondered at the Arabic word of endearment, which could mean anything from a friend to a beloved, telling myself to believe at the former. Though I was resisting my attraction for him, I did not want it to progress at a speed with which I would be out of depth.

That night was a long one. I was unable to sleep, my mind going over the happenings of the past few days and recollecting about Samarthya's life, and some time during the night, I drifted off to sleep.

The next morning I was off to some more sightseeing on my own, as S was attending his office. It had been decided that we would be leaving on Sunday for Aswan to see the temples at Abu Simbel.

I was going to explore the Islamic Cairo visiting the Salah-El-Din citadel, a massive structure built by Salah-al-Din more popularly known as Saladin to the Christian crusaders. By ten in the morning a taxi had deposited me to my destination. Mohammed Ali mosque rising above the citadel is the most prominent and recognizable amongst the Cairo mosques. It's domes and minarets have been on the Cairo skyline since the mid 1900's.

Exploring the mosque was a pleasure and awe inspiring. It's massive domes were covered with tin and some how reminded me of the blue mosque in Turkey. The inside of the mosque was truly beautiful with gilded ceilings and ornate chandeliers. I found the brass clock tower in the mosque to be amazing. The French ruler Louis Phillip had presented the clock to Mohammed Ali, a former commander of the Ottoman army. This was in exchange for the obelisk that presently adorns the Palace du Concorde in Paris.

The mosque of Ibn Tulun built in 879 AD is the oldest and largest mosque in Cairo. I was impressed by it's simplicity and according to my trip advisor guide; it's the only mosque with a minaret that can be climbed giving a panoramic view of Cairo. I could not gather the courage to do the same, although not exactly afraid of heights, I did not relish being so high up.

It was almost three in the afternoon and I was absolutely famished and decided to experiment with the street foods of Cairo.

I followed my travel guide and decided to have "Koshary" the ultimate comfort food made of wheat grains; rice, chickpeas and a variety of shapes of wheat pasta garnished with a mild tomato sauce and browned onions. One can add vinegar or additional spicy sauce to enliven it. This apparently can be called the national dish of Egypt.

So there I was with my bowl of koshary at a street side café, relishing the taste and also ruing the carbs that were going to play havoc with my increasing girth!

Being in Egypt and not having falafel was like a crime, so I committed the sin of taking my gluttonous crimes further. Then throwing caution to the winds, I decided to go all the way and had the Basbausa a sweet made from semolina flour that is popular across the Arab world. It is cheap and the best way to get a burst of sugary highness. Totally satiated and almost ready to fall off with tiredness, I took a taxi back to the hotel.

It was nearing six in the evening, when I reached the hotel, and I went straight to my room for that much needed cleansing and freshening bath.

I was sitting in front of the mirror brushing my hair and every now and then my eyes veered towards the telephone, my ears hyper tuned to a possible ring. Who was I kidding? It was not a call that I expected from my family and feelings of guilt assailed me. I may not be having the best of the marriage but I was a responsible mother. My sons, though grown up, were used to my maternal molly coddling, having long ceased to argue with me that they were grown up men and could look after themselves without daily intervention from my end. I realized that I had not called them since yesterday and with trepidation dialed my elder son Atharv's number. A few rings later, I could hear a recorded voice asking me to leave a message, making it easier for me to assuage my guilt feelings.

It is so strange how we women so easily give in to guilt pangs when we feel that we have slipped up on our expected behavior.

I guess we have been programmed to be the epitome of goodliness and any deviations are the marks of a woman, who has not been successful in managing her home and her career. This is the case with many of the women of this generation.

Men are so matter-of-fact about such issues and I guess it is we who have to change, reducing the unnecessary pressure we build upon ourselves.

I contemplated going down for dinner but that elusive call took away the mood and with an almost abject apathy I ordered room service.

It was late in the night around 11ish, I was still tossing and turning around in the bed. My treacherous body was in conflict with my mind.

I was almost going to call Samarthya when a message beeped on my mobile. I noticed with an almost exultant pleasure that it was a message from S. He had written that he was sorry that we could not catch up on dinner due to some urgent work, which he needed to get over with, before we left for Aswan.

I was secretly happy that S felt guilty because I don't think we had made any plans for having dinner that night and yet he cared enough to apologize for the same. We women can be devious sometimes in making the men in our lives feel guilty especially when it suits us.

CHAPTER 6

We were catching the late afternoon flight to Aswan for our trip to Abu Simbel. I was meeting Samarthya at the Cairo airport as he was coming in straight from an early morning meeting from the office.

I reached the airport well in time. Samarthya had still not arrived and having completed my check-in formalities without any hitch, I went window-shopping. My heart was not in my favorite activity and time and again my eyes were glancing off the dial of the watch.

I was very restless so I went to the departure gate and sat there waiting for S. I was getting a little jittery wondering whether he was going to make it to the flight or had some thing happened and he had cancelled his trip.

My mind was whirring with all these unanswered queries and I took out my cellphone from my handbag, when a laconic and endearingly familiar voice drawled, "Madam you have dropped your passport."

"I don't want you to get into another crisis, otherwise I will become habituated to rescuing you."

I was so relieved to see Samarthya that I did not even pick up my fallen passport. He picked it up and safely placed it in my bag.

"Serena, Serena, sweetheart what would you do if I was not around," and he gently patted my flushed cheeks.

I blurted out that I thought he was not going to come and was held up due to some problem in his office and thus gave away how disappointed I would be, if he was not there on the trip with me.

"Thank you sweetheart for your concern for me and trust me, nothing was going to make me miss this trip with you," saying this, S pulled me in his arms and placed a light kiss on the top of my head.

All these words of endearments and his display of affection had me in a love trance. I was basking in this display of affection by S.

Soon we had boarded the plane and the almost hour and a half flight time to Aswan passed in no time with S regaling me with some funny situations he had encountered interacting with people across the world.

It was almost eight in the evening when we reached the luxurious boutique hotel.

It was an awkward moment when the reception staff greeted me as Mrs. Singh but I waived off the embarrassment and told them that I had a separate booking in the name of Serena Khanna. In my heart I was dying of mortification at their blunder and was wondering what the staff may be thinking about the two of us.

I guess they must be used to such situations, probably they must be thinking we were strange, since we had separate rooms though our body language spoke of an intimate story.

Having completed the formalities, we went to our respective rooms to freshen up before dinner.

The room was elegantly done up in mid eastern décor and was the epitome of understated luxury. What blew me apart was the bathroom with an open skylight and a side that opened in to a small cul de sac of a vibrant green garden. My very own private mini tropical garden, I could just saunter out of my bathroom, sit on the small table and chair, sipping my tea or reading my book with absolute privacy. For once I was late coming down for dinner and found S waiting in the lobby area reading a newspaper.

He merely looked at me with one raised eyebrow as if enquiring if all was ok. I just nodded and we went in for dinner, which was amazing, like everything else in this place. After a post dinner cup of tea, S and I parted company at the door of my room.

It was to be an early start at four am the next morning. The journey to Abu Simbel by road was almost 300 kilometers. It was a tough journey through the desert, and a terrorist attack risk from a neighboring country made it compulsory for all vehicles to travel in a convoy with armed military escort.

We took the early morning trip to make sure that we were back in Aswan by the evening, as there weren't many hotels with good facilities at Abu Simbel.

Early morning we were on our way to Abu Simbel ensconced in a luxurious air-conditioned mini bus, which was a blessing, because the outside temperature was extremely hot and dry. I had decided to wear a simple linen shift dress in pale pistachio, to off set the blinding sunlight and heat, taking care to liberally doff myself with sunscreen.

S was wearing a pair of beige shorts with a sky blue linen shirt and as always managed to look cool and in control. On board, he declared that he was going off to sleep, to catch up on the much- needed rest that he had been missing. It was going to be a long, almost three-hour journey, and I decided to read about the temples at Abu Simbel.

The temples of Abu Simbel are two massive rock temples made by Rameses II in the 13th century BC, as a lasting monument to himself and his queen Nefertari celebrating his victory in the Battle of Kadesh. These temples are a part of the UNESCO world heritage site known as the Nubian Monuments and are situated on the western bank of Lake Nasser. In 1968 the entire temple was relocated on a manmade hill, as it would have submerged under the waters of the artificial Lake Nasser, which was formed when the High Dam was made on the River Nile. The whole process cost an astronomical $ 40 million at that time.

A team of archaeologists and engineers had carefully cut up the entire site with each block weighing on an average of 20 tons. They had transported and then reassembled them on the new higher site. An astounding feat by no means, and today the whole world has the pleasure of seeing this magnificent temple complex. The more I read, the more eager I was getting to set my sights on the temple.

I looked up from my book, and saw Samarthya sleeping. He looked so vulnerable in his sleep. I took advantage of the same by feasting my eyes on the countenance that was fast becoming something more, than what my heart wanted to admit.

My fingers itched to trace the sensual line of his lips and that one winging curve of his eyebrow. So engrossed was I in watching his lips, that I missed seeing S watching me through slitted eyes.

His right hand snaked up suddenly taking my left hand in his, guiding it to his lips, helping my now limp hand to trace his lip line. I was like a fly caught in spider's web, unable to do anything but just stare like a zombie.

Then he slowly kissed the tips of each finger and I almost reared up with carnal pleasure when he sucked my index finger. I looked around furtively to see if our neighbors on the other side of the aisle, a staid old British couple, were watching this erotic display. I heaved a sigh of relief noting that they were fast asleep.

S murmured, "I knew they were! But even if they were awake, it would not have deterred me and anyways, this is harmless."

I tried pulling my hand away but S held it more tightly till I gave up. He asked me in a husky voice if I liked what I had seen and touched, and would I want my lips to explore the same?

"Please Samarthya," I implored with him.

"Please what, Serena? Kiss you or you want to kiss me," he asked wickedly and mercifully let go of my hand.

I looked out of the window and a vista of desolate sand scape, harsh and unforgiving, was all that could be seen as far as the eye could see. How much like my life it was, unending and lifeless. The man sitting next to me showed me a contrast that I could easily fall for, though I knew it was a mirage.

We were passing by an oasis, which seemed to be dying as if unable to bear the savage inflictions of the desert. After a long time, words came out from the prisons of my mind, which I had locked and thrown the keys off to some unknown corner. I pulled out my smart phone and started jotting down the words which were unfurling.

> A desert pool long lost under the
> shifting sands
> Tufts of withered grass like a tattered
> carpet await a footfall
> A grove of dying date palms
> Swing drunkenly in the desert wind
> A lingering death is like dying over and
> over again.

Yes, did I want to die again and again or break free?

"Serena, be honest and admit that your marriage is over," I said to myself.

My upbeat mood at the start of the journey plunged a few hundred feet down, pulling me in an abyss of despair.

"Hey, sweet heart, what's wrong? You seem to be holding all the problems of the world on your delicate shoulders! Why are you looking so sad and distraught?" Samarthya's concerned voice broke through my wall of misery.

It was as if a dam of emotions had broken apart and I just fell limply into his arms crying out, "Oh Samarthya."

I was grateful to him for not probing any further and just letting me quietly lie in the sanctuary of his arms.

One day I would tell him my story, but what good was it going to do!

Lying there in the comfort of his arms, lulled me into a false sense of security, not realizing when I dozed off to sleep.

A gentle pressure of a kiss on my lips had me snuggling deeper into S's arms. Samarthya gently shook me and murmured, "Darling, wake up, we have reached."

I sat up a little groggy, wondering whether I had been kissed by Samarthya. Had I actually heard the word of endearment or had it been in my pleasant dream!

"Wake up sleeping beauty! We are at your revered destination," these words from Samarthya woke me up for proper.

I quickly dove into my handbag for my hairbrush, giving my hair a quick stroke. I took out my small vanity mirror, wanting to retouch the lipstick which I always inevitably ended up eating after some time.

I saw S watching me intently with a look I could not decipher, his eyes dark and inscrutable and my hands faltered in their job of applying the lipstick.

"Stop staring at me Samarthya," I laughed trying to break the magic spell of his eyes and the tension fraught moments. All S did at that moment was take the lipstick tube from my hand and said huskily, "I want to kiss you Serena," pulling my unresisting body in to his arms.

A shiver of pleasure ran through my body at the fleeting touch of his sensuous lips. As S deepened the kiss, I had no volition, our tongues entwined and sucking, as if drawing out the very essense of our being. My hands reaching out to embrace him, wanting to feel the broad strength of his chest.

It was the, "How sweet and romantic, Arthur darling, to see this handsome couple so much in love with each other," chiming of our elderly British neighbour across the bus aisle to her husband that had me scrambling apart from S.

I was blushing furiously and Samarthya turned to give a devastating smile to the woman. He drawled, "She is a witch! She has me in her spell!"

I don't know what spell I had on him but the British woman was surely bewitched, smiling widely, having been the beneficiary of Samarthya's deadly charm.

Soon S and I were part of our tour group being led to the temple complex of Abu Simbel. We were all cautioned to remain with the group and not wander off as this was a time bound tour. We had to be back on the bus for our return journey to Aswan.

This time around S did not wait for me to trip but held my hand right at the outset. It was as if we were a couple, and a very loving one at that, because at our age I don't think many husbands and wives go walking around holding hands. At least Jeh my husband and I had not done this for a very very long time. I was not complaining, but enjoying this feeling of possessiveness that Samarthya exhibited towards me.

Soon we were engrossed, listening and soaking in the history of the amazing temples.

The great temple at Abu Simbel was completed in the reign of Rameses the Great around 1265BC and is dedicated to the gods Amun, Ra-Horakhty and Ptah. The smaller temple is dedicated to the Goddess Hathor personified by queen Nefertari, the most beloved wives of Rameses. Standing at the foot of the colossal statutes of Rameses, we were humbled by their beauty and grandeur. I was left wondering how thousands of years ago, without any benefit of technology, these time lasting tributes were made. I wonder if any of the modern day monuments would withstand the ravages of time and bedazzle our future generations.

What impressed S and me the most, was the belief that the axis of the temple was positioned in a way that the sun's rays, on October 22 and February 22, would penetrate the inner sanctuary and sculptures except the statue of Ptah the god of the underworld, which would always be in darkness.

The next few hours passed quickly and after a lunch break, we followed our guide towards the parking lot where our bus was parked. A sizeable number of the tourist buses had already left and more were leaving as it was safer to travel back to Aswan before night time.

We should also have been leaving except that a group of six tourists from our bus were missing. The tour guide was franctically trying to call his head office to find out the contact numbers of any of the missing people and we could see that he was having no luck, and our departure was getting delayed.

Finally a team of young men from our group and the guide decided to go search for them. All of us decided we should wait for them as there were women and a young child in the group of tourists from China, though they had been callous in having no regard for the time and comfort of the rest of us.

It was almost two hours before the errant group was found and brought back. On top, their limited English made it difficult to understand why they had delayed all of us.

This was not the end of our troubles! We were advised by the local police authorities that it would now be unsafe for us to travel back to Aswan. There had been some rebel activities on the border areas, thus forcing us to spend the night at Abu Simbel.

All of us were most upset with the stopover and the additional expense that would have to be borne by us as the tour agency refused to bear the cost and if looks could kill, the Chinese tourists would have been dead!

In all this fiasco, Samarthya was at his coolest best. He told me to stop getting hyper and accept the situation and move on, and make the best out of this unfortunate episode.

Soon we were taken to the hotel which had some rooms available and I found to my dismay that I would have to share the room with Samarthya as the group thought we were a couple. Even if I would have wanted a separate room, there was none available. The only choice I had, was to spend the night sitting in the lobby. This would incur speculations from our fellow tourists and the hotel staff and I would end up looking ridiculous.

Samarthya as usual was cool as a cucumber and just gave me an inscrutable look and walked off towards the lift lobby. I had no choice but to follow him.

I wonder if I could explain how strung up I was. I was experiencing a feeling of fear, of a situation where I would not be able to resist Samarthya at such close quarters. The sensual feelings of my body were not in sync with my reluctant mind and this was not exactly comforting.

Tortured with these conflicting thoughts, I found myself in the largish room and looked around and with relief noticed a comfortable couch. I immediately decided it was going to be my abode for the night. I saw S watching me with an amused look in his eyes and teasingly offered that the bed was large enough and we could share it. He said he would keep to his corner of the bed unless of course I could not bear to resist him.

Also, I was well aware that he always helped damsels in distress especially prettty ones like me, and would be glad to offer his services.

I knew he was trying to diffuse the palpable tension in the room and gave a strained smile to him.

I assured him that I would be fine on the couch and it was only for a night.

Since we did not have any change of clothes and any toiletries, we did the best with what ever the hotel had provided. S suggested to me to freshen up first. We would order for room service since we had had a tiring day.

I took a quick shower and rewore my now crumpled linen dress after liberally spraying myself with Palomo Picasso perfume hoping to feel fresh in the sweat stained clothes. S looked so cool, the whole episode having no impact on his personna. I guess these media people were used to adverse field jobs and knew how to make the best of the circumstances.

After our dinner, I was almost drooping off to sleep, the tension of the day seeping out of me. I had sort of got comfortable with S in the room, considering he had behaved impeccably, with not even a word of any teasing or otherwise which could unnerve me.

I took the extra sheet and a pillow from the bed and lay down on the couch though Samarthya did offer to use it.

I laughed and turned him down saying my size was more conducive for the couch rather than his tall and masculine frame.

He did not have an inch of fat on his tall frame despite being at an age, when it is easy for both men and women to start piling fat, if they were not careful about some sort of physical activity and eating the right kind of food.

Well I was the living example of how difficult it was to fight the losing battle of the bulge. My husband, Jeh was very fit, and my mother-in-law a very figure conscious woman, was a sort of high priestess of health in the Delhi society.

This did not make it any easier for me and I was sometimes quite upset by her barbs on my fulsome figure which was more a result of heredity than any bad habits on my part. Initially her one remark could push me in to the doldrums but over the years I had developed a thick skin and I was quite happy with the way I was, and looked.

When Samarthya had remarked that he liked me just the way I was, my happiness and self confidence which were high with his attentions, took another level and I was almost floating with pleasure.

"What are you thinking? I can see that something is pleasing you," Samarthya's voice cut through my pleasant musings. I merely nodded nothing and settled in my couch, drawing the sheet right upto my chin as if protecting my self from S.

"Goodnight Serena, I am switching off all the lights, or do you need a night lamp? " asked Samarthya.

I told him I was fine without any night lamp, and as soon as the room plunged into darkness, I gingerly removed my under garments under the sheet. I could not have slept wearing them, as I feel very claustrophobic. Once I am in bed, I can only be in my soft boxer shorts and a sleeveless tee. I decided I would be up before Samarthya and be safely dressed and thinking so, I drifted off to sleep.

The desert stretched for miles around, everywhere I looked, all that I could see was unending dunes. The sun shone relentlessly bright, blinding my eyes.
My body was burning in the searing heat and I was faint with thirst. I lurched on drunkenly, my feet sinking in the sand. I had no clue where to go and could feel the panic rising in me. Suddenly my tired and dejected eyes saw a shimmering body of water and palm trees! An oasis!! I almost whimpered in relief. My body suffused with a newfound energy, I started to run towards it, falling once on all my fours and somehow picking my self again and running towards it.
But the oasis seemed to move away from me with each step that I took towards it, teasing me, taunting me, "Serena come to me, I will save you, give you the life you

have been wanting! Come before it's too late and you are dead," a voice chanted again and again in my head.

I kept on stumbling and running towards the oasis never reaching it. My body gave up it's fight and I cried out again and again asking for help, my hands and legs flailing in the air.

I felt myself held strongly in a pair of arms and I struggled more, trying to free myself, whimpering in fright, asking to be let free, pleading with the unseen entity, "Please help me find my way in life! I am lost, I will die in this lonely desert! Please help me."

"Shush baby, wake up, you are having a nightmare, darling I am here, don't worry nothing is going to happen to you, I promise," Samarthya's gentle and coaxing voice penetrated thru the haze of my terrifying dream.

I started crying when the realization struck, that it had been a dream and not the real life-like experience I had been having in my dream.

"Oh Samarthya," I cried out, holding on to him and letting go of the dam of emotions I had been holding on to, behind a façade of contrived happiness.

For a long time, I sat there in his arms sobbing softly. He also did not stop me, letting me rid my self of the pain that had been wracking my soul and body for a long time. Occasionally he would kiss the top of my head with a soft gentle kiss making me cry out in more anguish.

The storm was over. I was totally drained out and sat in the dark with Samarthya holding me in the strong circle of his arms. I just let go of myself, falling limply against him as if giving up on life itself. At that moment

S, just picked me up effortlessly and strode towards the bed and gently placed me on it. I protested weakly, to let go of me.

"Serena, I am not going to do anything to you darling, you just need to sleep comfortably on a bed," saying this Samarthya placed me gently on the bed and turned to go away. He said that he would sleep on the couch.

I reached out for him in the darkness, on being parted from the warmth of his comforting body.

"Don't leave me Samarthya, Please can you hold me, till I go to sleep," my voice a pitiful quiver.

"Yes, my darling, I am here, dont worry," saying this, Samarthya lay besides me after tucking me in the bedsheet. It was then I realized with great shame that I was almost naked, my dress having bunched up high up to my thighs. True to his words, S just held me in his arms while I almost immediately fell in to a deep sleep, as a result of the sapping emotional drama of a dream that I had dreamt.

It was early morning around four, when I woke up with a confused daze to find my self in bed with Samarthya. His one arm lay heavily on my body holding me. I remembered the nightmare and the circumstance of my being on the bed with him, vaguely remembering with shame my pleading with him to stay and hold me.

A soft glow of the night lamp illuminated his face, which was without the usual sardonic expression which he always favoured as if ridiculing the world for it's thinkings! The sensual line of his lips, tempting me to outline them with my finger and the face ruggedly handsome and unshaven, made my heart beat with an unknown fear.

A slight movement from S made me quickly shut my eyes, not wanting him to know that I was awake and watching him.

A feather touch of his lips on my eyelids made me realize that he knew I had been looking at him. I kept my eyes closed, my insides curling up with an unknown desire, my body tense, waiting for an assault that I knew, I would not be able to fight back. I felt, Samarthya like an eagle was waiting to swoop down and carry me off.

"Sleeping Beauty, Wake up"! He whispered hoarsely in my ear. I turned to get off the bed but he threw his leg over my thighs and with one hand pulled me towards him, trapping me to his chest.

"Please Samarthya," I whispered.

"Please Samarthya what? Say, please Samarthya hold me, make love to me, make me yours"! S whispered back.

All I could hear was the pounding of two hearts and the laboured breathing of two bodies, waiting for that moment when they would ignite and get burnt by a smouldering fire.

S moved over me crushing me with his weight and cupped my face with both his hands, dropping fleeting kisses on my eyes, moving to the tip of my nose, my chin and finally unable to hold back his passion, he took control of my lips. His lips ground against mine, forcing them open. His tongue inside my mouth was doing things that made my insides curl up with passion. I was immobile under his excruciatingly pleasurable body weight with absolutely no thoughts of resistance.

I don't know when my hands reached out and gripped his smooth broad shoulders holding unto them like I was drowning in the sea of his passion. I kissed him back with an equal intensity, matching him a kiss for his kiss, frantically kissing his brows, his eyes and sucking the tips of his ears.

My dress was like a barrier to the touch of his skin and Samarthya tugged it off my head and I unashamedly helped him remove the constricting garment. It was as if a blaze erupted, when skin touched skin and we were annihilated in the fiery passion.

Our hands greedily explored each other and could not have our fill. The last straw to my total surrender was when Samarthya gently cradled my breast, sucking it hungrily, and then all was lost.

In the passion filled haze, I realized that it was my voice which was moaning and pleading with S to make love to me.

"Serena you are driving me crazy, darling! Are you sure, because if you don't stop me now, I won't be able to hold myself back," S groaned and rolling down, pulled me on top of him, as if giving me the chance to move away from all this.

I was past any coherent thinking and having touched Samarthya, I did not have the restraint to hold my self back anymore. All I did was bend down and kiss him right on his lips and then his dark brooding sexy eyes, giving him my answer.

Finally unable to bear any more of the sweet agony, S immersed himself in me with a strong thrust of his impressive manhood and I almost reared up with the pleasurable assault.

Then started the pagan rhythm, which has been enacted ever since there was a man and a woman on this earth. Every thrust of his took me to a new height, finally unable to bear the sweet pain; my body gave up to a shattering climax. S also reached his peak shooting his seeds in my very core, rearing back with a raw wild cry of my name. At that moment, I think I almost fell in love with S.

It was true I loved this man! I had fallen in love, with the clichéd, "love at first sight," statement coming true for me!

I had been denying it, telling myself that no such thing existed. Finally what my mind had denied, my body demonstrated by telling him over and over that I wanted him and loved him. For a long time we just lay there, our bodies love soaked and tired.

He turned towards me and gently gathered me in his arms and there was an unspoken question in his eyes. I smiled and gave my answer by gently kissing his lips. The devil that he was, he smiled and told me that I was his now, completely.

It was the aftermath of this passionate folly I had committed, that was going to wrack me with an infinite guilt. I realized this, but as if another doppelganger was lying on that bed with a wanton abandon and not the staid me, who had always lived her life for others.

Tired, we just drifted off to sleep knowing that we would have to be up in the next few hours for our return journey to Aswan.

On the way back, I felt like another me. I felt so complete, reveling in the desire of a man who was becoming so dear to me. I felt almost in the throes of love and on the journey back to Aswan I was lost in my dreams leaning comfortably against Samarthya. It was as if all barriers of inhibitions were broken down and I almost felt proprietorial towards him, though deep down I knew he and I were both tied down to marriages, which were not ideal. Actually for one moment a surge of panic rose in me, was I not assuming that his marriage was not ideal?

S had never spoken about it or indicated about any discord.

What if he was a Casanova preying on emotionally gullible stupid women who would easily catapult to his clever machinations.

But then I was being selfish, had I ever indicated blatantly to Samarthya that my marriage was in a precarious state. He could be having an equally disreputable opinion about myself, as a woman who was promiscuous!

After sharing such an intimate act I decided that I could not go ahead with this relationship unless I shared with Samarthya the reason for my abandon, as I did not want him to view me in a negative light.

We reached Aswan in early evening and went to our respective rooms for the much-needed bath and change of clothes. My clothes were pretty crumpled and disreputable.

I took time deciding to run my bath and soak my self in some decadent bath salts. I also loved the beautiful bathroom, which opened into a small tropical garden, my own private Eden. I immersed my self in the warm scented waters and the aromatic candles that I had lit in the bathroom took me to a state of absolute ecstasy.

I was in a state of languid stupor, my body relieved of the physical and mental tension that I had been experiencing for the past few days. After having been in the bath for almost an hour, I got out and dried myself. I wore a bathrobe and decided to sit out in my tiny garden. It was late evening and I helped myself to a glass of red wine which had been provided courtesy our luxury hotel.

The chime of the doorbell got me scrambling to the room, I had forgotten all about the dinner date at 9 pm with Samarthya. I hurriedly looked at my watch, relieved to note that there was still half an hour to spare and I would be ready by that time. It could not be him at the door, more likely the housekeeping staff with a replacement ironing board I had requested. There seemed to be a problem with the one in the room.

I opened the door to find S, bewildered to see him standing there and more so since I was almost in a state of dishabille with nothing underneath my bathrobe.

"Won't you invite me to come in?" Asked Samarthya.

Embarrassed, I muttered that I was about to get ready and would he mind waiting in the lobby for me. S walked in and shut the door, gathering me in his arms said, "Why should I wait in the lobby darling, why, are you feeling shy of me?"

I felt a fury of color rush through my face on being reminded of the passionate encounter I had with him. I was quiet and S looked at me with the question repeated in his eyes. I could not bear to look in to his dark smoky eyes thus revealing the turmoil I was experiencing.

S slowly lowered his lips on to mine placing a gentle teasing kiss, his arms drawing me closer to his broad chest.

My traitorous body betrayed it's aroused state and my hands unbeknown to me reached out and encircled S drawing him closer. This was a signal that broke our restraint.

S ground his lips against mine, murmuring, "Darling I need you, I cannot keep my self away from you. Please, only you can make me sane again."

After this we were lost in a carnal haze, kissing, petting and stroking each other like two starved people who have found food after many days.

It was only some time later I realized that I had been divested of my robe and S was also without his shirt. I felt ashamed of my passion, which I did not know I was capable of. I was this wanton woman who was ready to do all with her man.

I whispered to S asking him should we not be going for our dinner, and he retorted hoarsely,

"I am hungry for you Serena and f… the food," and lifted me in his arms and went into the garden adjoining my bathroom about which I had told him. Then started a journey where there was no end to the bodily pleasures he inflicted on my willing body and both of us gave ourselves totally to each other, body and soul.

S picked me up again, even as I protested that I was heavy and all this lifting he had been doing, could hurt his back.

"Madam I am not an old man yet, I can lift you and run also! Only a few steps!" S winked at me, laying me gently on the bed.

It was late and we were in no mood to go down for dinner so we called room service for some sandwiches and a bottle of red wine. We finished the full bottle and I devoured the sandwiches, as I was famished. The wine had made me feel like I was floating and I sat comfortably ensconced in Samarthya's arms, my head on his chest, as if it was the most natural thing to do.

CHAPTER 7

"My wife and I have not had a real marriage for the past many years!"

This was the first time, I had heard S speak about his personal life and was shocked by this sudden statement from him at this moment of time. I had prodded him some time back and he had avoided the topic.

He told me that his wife had been the daughter of a career diplomat, whose postings had taken them all over the globe. Maheka had everything going for her, right from the time she was born. The life of a person born with the proverbial silver spoon, except in her case, more like a golden spoon.

She, being the only child, her parents had doted on her and given her the best in life. She had graduated from a prestigious US university and had started working as a field reporter for a renowned news agency.

Her parents wanted their blue-blooded daughter to have the best in life and that included having a life partner who was equally matched in terms of social and educational qualities.

Samarthya laughed cynically, telling that Maheka, their beautiful and talented daughter had done the unpardonable sin of falling in love, and that too, with a struggling reporter who had yet to establish his name in the upper echelons of the news world.

Worse, according to her parents, was the fact, that he was a village hick from some God- forsaken village of India.

Fortunately, he said, his mother had passed away; otherwise his simple and stoic mother would have never expressed to him the pain of having a daughter-in-law and her parents who would have looked down on the fiercely independent woman. Her expectations of having a daughter-in-law, who would be more of a daughter and friend to her, would have been shattered.

"How and where did you meet her?" I asked.

They had met during an assignment in Eastern Europe. He had gone there to cover war genocide and she was apparently covering the same, on behalf of her news agency. Most of the news agencies' reporters were staying in the only whole and functioning hotel.

In the evening he had gone down to the hotel bar for the much-needed drink to momentarily forget the horrific scenes of the war crimes. As a reporter he was learning to detach himself from the realities, without being insensitive. It was needed, he said, otherwise we would be mental wrecks considering the things we see and have to report about.

While he was chatting with a fellow journalist, he had heard female laughter, full of gay and abandon, and it was with surprise and amusement he had looked back to see the woman with such joie de vivre in this dismal and mind sapping atmosphere.

"There she was, the most beautiful woman I had seen. She was talking to a man, her hands waving around emphasizing a point she was making, and again she laughed!" said Samarthya.

"Serena, I fell in love at first sight, if any thing like love is true, which of course I now know, is an extinct dinosaur."

Hearing S say that, made my heart sink a million miles and I felt jealous of Maheka who had made S fall in love with her at the first sight.

Had I not done the same folly of falling in love with S at the first sight? I had been denying it all along and now, hearing Samarthya's view on love, made me feel worse.

"I was drawn to her and fates conspired to unite us. Our team photographer who was her friend, asked her to join us at the dinner table, where the whole lot of the news fraternity were gathered."

"She looked like a Latin American and had an accent, but when I was introduced to her, I realized that she was an Indian, Maheka Chauhan. I felt as if I had made an instant connect with her," S laughed cynically.

"We both got talking and were so inseparable, that the rest of my team teased me, asking me whether I had made a serious conquest. At that time I felt that I had found the one person who had been missing in my life. I was totally bowled over by the dark haired and vivacious beauty who was such a contrast to my serious personality. It was love at first sight for me and I think Maheka was equally taken in by me."

"The remaining free time, while we were in the country, were spent together, talking and finding about each other and in fact by the third day, we were lover's also," laughed Samarthya.

"Everything was on a fast forward button, it started with a bang and is now ending with a bang."

It was past midnight and Samarthya went on telling me his story and I was equally keen to know about him and his wife.

He told me that after their assignment was over, Maheka and he met in Delhi the following month. Her parents were based there. It had been fortunate because she was taking her annual vacations, as she worked out of the news agency's headoffice in New York.

That was also one of the issues that had bothered him, her being on the other side of the world. In the initial throes of passion and love, they had not given it much thought, taking the simplistic approach of handling it, when it came to that.

More over, both of them were travelling half the month, traversing distant corners of the world.

S also took a fortnight's break, which he had never taken in the last three years since being with the news agency. Maheka and he had been inseparable, causing her parents to sit up and question their daughter, who was the apple of their eyes.

She had never been that close in a relationship with a man. They wanted to know about Samarthya and invited him for dinner one evening. Her parent's snobbish attitude towards S's background, despite his present credentials and achievements in the news world, had been a shock to Maheka. She had thought highly of her parents and was most annoyed with them for their stuck-up attitude.

Her parents had very politely and indirectly made it clear to S, that despite his present position he was no match for their daughter who had had the best in life. They wondered whether he would be able to keep up with her expectations.

S said cynically, he did not know at that time, how true those words were going to be. At that moment he had politely ignored their barbs, respecting Maheka's parents and understanding their concern, as he had grown up with the sound values of respecting the elders. This had been ground into him by his simple and fiercely independent mother.

He was clear he was going to marry Maheka and would do what ever, to make her happy.

Maheka had told him that after he had left that night, for the first time in her life, she and her parents had been at loggerheads. They were most unhappy about her choice of a life partner, warning her that they were mismatched in their social and mental standing.

In retrospect he would agree with her parents that indeed Maheka and he had been mismatched as far as a mental connect was concerned! It had indeed been a marriage in haste and regret in leisure thing for them.

They had got married in a civil ceremony by the end of her vacations. Her parents had refused to attend the court wedding and no amount of tears and tantrums from Maheka had softened their stance.

The civil ceremony had been a simple affair with Maheka's best friend and her husband as witnesses.

She had looked ravishingly beautiful in a red sari and that had made him feel proud that she was his and they were so much in love with each other and would overcome any barriers in their life.

Post the wedding Maheka had made one last attempt to call her parents but they had not yielded and this had hurt her deeply.

She was unable to comprehend their stubborn stance, when all her life they had acquiesced to all her demands.

They had flown off to Bali for a one -week honeymoon, as they both could not take more leave. That one-week, according to S, had been the most idyllic time of their lives, discovering each other more deeply.

They had decided for some time Maheka would continue with her job at the New York office and both of them would try to get a transfer or a job, each open to a change in location. This was a good positive start to their commitment to each other.

According to S, Maheka and he were lucky because six months down, there was a suitable opening in the news agency where S was working, in Delhi.

Maheka with her excellent credentials and experience managed to get the job, though, she did express moments of unhappiness in leaving her beloved New York.

S had teasingly promised her that they would make a yearly trip to her beloved Mecca till she overcame her love affair with it.

It came as a surprise to Samarthya, to learn that Maheka had made inroads with regard to her relationship with her parents. He had felt a little strange that she had not confided in him. But he was happy for her that they had at least started talking to her.

Her parents had been happy with her decision of not quitting her job in New York till she found a suitable opening in India.

Maheka's parents had finally relented, as she had been sure of, and called them for dinner. Though the occasion had been rather stilted, it was a start to their coming to know each other.

S ironically stated that in the end, he had become closer to Maheka's parents than her, and it was he, they turned to, in their hours of need.

They had settled in their married life easily. S had been reluctant to stay with her parents. However Maheka and her parents had worn him down to shifting with them in their posh central Delhi home.

He had felt it as an intrusion in his private life. The saving grace had been their independent apartment on the first floor. The times either of them were in Delhi, they would end up having their meals with her parents and thus the modern kitchen in the apartment rarely saw any cooking being done except S making his morning cup of tea.

In a way he agreed that it had been a good arrangement leaving them both the time and freedom to pursue their hectic careers. It was easy leaving the mundane tasks of looking after a home to Maheka's more than capable mother, who ran the house with clockwork precision.

Samarthya mused that some times, during those days it had seemed to him that he was not in a home but a hotel where everything was taken care of and he just came and went according to his own convenience.

The times he and Maheka were together in Delhi, they partied a lot, as Maheka was very gregarious and loved socializing. Those initial years were without any major hiccups because there had been no responsibilities.

Thus the initial few years had been a whirl of passion and hectic work assignments. Sometimes they managed to get work as a team but mostly they were away from each other for a large part of the year. They took this as a repercussion of their career goals.

After nearly five years, Samarthya, tired of his hectic life, wanted to slow down, and be in the newsroom rather than traipsing distant corners of the world. He discussed with Maheka the idea of doing this and also if they could start a family. They were both in their late twenties and he felt this was the right time for them to slow down for a while and start a family and then once the child was sufficiently old enough, either could pursue their careers to the next level.

For once, he found ready support from Maheka's parents who had been advising her to start a family.

She had been reluctant, as her career as a journalist was going great places. She had finally capitulated to impassioned reasoning from her mother, who pointed out that till date, Maheka had no problems regarding the running of her home. Her mother told her that she could help in the upbringing of a grandchild, with some efficient help. This would not have been possible later due to her advancing years and diminished abilities.

"The honeymoon period of our marriage was finally over," said Samarthya.

He told me that Maheka's pregnancy had been full of complications. This had caused her to be on complete bed rest for the last four months of her pregnancy. The constant bouts of nausea and vomiting, had added to her misery. Instead of accepting and enjoying the enforced period of inactivity, Maheka had become very short tempered and moody. Her doctor had also forbidden any kind of stress, so working out of home or literally the bed had been out of question.

Samarthya had understood and empathized with her sentiments and moods and tried to spend as much time as was possible with her. Even risking refusing an important overseas assignment towards the final days of her confinement. Fortunately for him, his boss had understood and he had been able to get away with it.

At times, he felt that Maheka almost accused him of getting her in such a miserable state of mind and body. But he had ignored her tantrums like an indulgent parent and reassured her that everything would be back to what she wanted, once the baby was born.

There were times when she would be very happy and exhibit feelings of maternal pride at the baby that had been created by both of them. Those according to S were some sane moments in the tension filled period of her pregnancy. They had spent time choosing names and had decided if a daughter was born she would be named Sukanya Tara, the second name in the memory of his late mother. On the name of a son, they would never end up having an agreement, as if deep down they knew a daughter was what they wanted and were going to get.

On a windy early December morning, their daughter Sukanya Tara Singh had arrived in this world, much to the relief of everyone, especially Samarthya.

Maheka for a few months was given to the pleasures of motherhood, devoting herself totally to looking after Tara, the name all had taken to calling her.

She had also decided to take a break from work until she decided she wanted to get back to it. Samarthya said that he had not pressurized her to do the same.

Maheka's parents felt it to be the right decision and also inadvertently helped S because he wanted Maheka to be with their daughter during her first few years.

"But that was being very unfair on Maheka! Why is it always the woman who has to make the sacrifices," I protested.

"Serena in hindsight I think you are right! But at that moment she had already been away from work for some time. The emotional and physical turmoil that she had faced during the pregnancy, was another factor and this break would have helped her to get back to her normal self and additionally give her a chance to bond with the baby," said Samarthya.

S went on with his story, telling me that two years flew past as if in a second. Tara was turning out to be a beautiful child and Maheka, though a good and caring mother, was slowly getting restless wanting to get back to her career, as if tired of playing the role of a mother.

S felt that it was but natural, considering she had been a bright, much in demand journalist.

They discussed and mutually agreed that Maheka would initially free lance for some time giving her a transition period, during which she could switch back to a full time career.

All would have gone well, but fate had some other plans for them! Maheka's mother, who had been a pillar of support during all those years, was taken seriously ill with a paralytic stroke.

Maheka, who had taken to doing freelance assignments, was suddenly burdened with the responsibility of looking after her parent, a growing child and the humdrum task of running a home.

Though there was an efficient fleet of help to take care of the household chores and her mother, it was still a lot of added responsibility.

All this suddenly put her career on the back burner and slowly but steadily Maheka started resenting the fact that it was her career that was being sacrificed.

Fights started happening every other day, with Maheka accusing him of not participating in the looking after of Tara. She said she was facing all the problems alone.

S said it was a false accusation. He was doing the best he could with his hectic career demands, helping Maheka as much as he could. He was taking care of Tara and her needs when he was back home from work.

But things did not get any better; in fact they went from bad to worse.

Finally Samarthya decided to quit his full time job and do free lancing till the time the problems at home got settled.

He and Maheka started freelancing to accommodate to each other's schedules thus making sure that all was hunky dory with them on the home front.

This went on till Tara was sent off to a boarding school in class one.

I almost cried out in protest, as to how they could have done this, and such a torture for a child at that tender age.

"Serena, at that point it seemed to be the best option, things were not bad but neither were they the best. Maheka had got more and more involved with her assignments and sometimes did not even consult, as they had mutually agreed, to make sure that one of them was always in the city. The daily arguments were taking a toll on our marriage and confusing Tara," said S.

"Tara's going away to the boarding school was at that time the best decision, but some how it did not bring our marriage back on track. Some link had broken. We were together, yet apart," Were Samarthya's sad words!

Samarthya told that he too went back to a full time newsroom career and Maheka continued to freelance, albeit with more time to her disposal now that Tara was away in a boarding school.

In the following years there were more issues, when Maheka was so busy with her work assignments travelling across the globe that she started missing important events in their daughter's life.

"On Tara's thirteenth birthday which is a landmark teenage event, Maheka had not been there. She was covering a more important news article in some country in South America despite Tara having requested her months' in advance. Even she had got used to her mother's absence more than her presence in her young life," S said bitterly.

He had been there for Tara more number of instances than he could remember, always covering up for Maheka's growing indifference towards her only child.

More arguments and fights would follow every such instance.

They had continued with this state of affairs for their daughter, who despite all the upheavals in her young life, had fortunately turned out to be a well -groomed mature young woman ready to embark on her higher education in a prestigious college in England.

S disclosed that in the past decade and a half, a whole lot of things had happened in their lives. Maheka's parents had passed away and slowly they had drifted apart. To the external world they were still a handsome and successful couple.

"I don't remember when was it last that I and Maheka had made love or spent a whole day together," S remarked indifferently.

"We had switched to sleeping in separate bedrooms a long time back, her excuse being that since we travelled and kept odd hours we would be disturbing each other."

"From separate bedrooms to a different man or men in her life, I don't know how and when it had happened. There had been a rumor, which had started when Maheka had been away on a longish assignment with one of her fellow correspondent, a rakishly handsome Turkish journalist, famous for both his media and off media exploits. He played both the fields with equal aplomb and Maheka seemed to have fallen for his charms."

After that, S said he kept on hearing various discreet rumors about his wife and it was now an open secret that their marriage was a sham.

He never confronted his wife about them because he did not care any more. Both led a life of their own, he finding solace in short-term affairs.

"So this is my life in a nutshell. To the outside world we are a successful and modern couple who are tolerant of each other's flings! But then appearances are deceptive," said S.

Thinking about the state of my own married life, I asked S, did he not think it better to get out of a relationship that was dead and was bringing no love or happiness to him and his wife.

He said at one point in life they had considered a mutual divorce, but then Tara's well being held them back. Also the fact that they were so engrossed in their careers, they thought it better to continue till either of them found the necessity of giving up on their marriage.

Plus there was the added advantage of warding off any serious advances from the opposite sexes if they continued to be married, as both of them were happy playing the field.

I found it strange and mechanical asking S, what about love and companionship? Did they not want it? Was it not ironical! Such a question coming from me!

He just laughed cynically and quoted a line from a song by Tina Turner, "What's love but a second hand emotion," and in my heart I agreed.

That song of Tina Turner always evoked sadness in me.

He said, over the years, he would not deny that he had short discreet affairs, more for fulfilling a physical need because he was done with any kind of emotional bonding.

S saw the look of pain and disappointment in Serena's eyes on hearing his words and rushed to take her in his arms. What was it about this woman that drew out the protective instinct in him?

Her dark eyes hid a deep pain that she was valiantly trying to hide under her guise of a confident woman. Right from day one, when she had fallen in his arms at the airport, he had wanted to nurture and protect her and yet at the same time he wanted to suppress the feelings she evoked, not wanting to give weightage to them.

"Serena darling, please, you are not a physical distraction for me. I treasure the time I spend with you," and saying this S kissed Serena gently on her face, dropping fleeting kisses on her eyes nose and forehead.

Then unable to hold back, he kissed her passionately on her lips, feverishly persuading them to open up and give an access to her very being.

Serena struggled with her emotions and finally gave up the losing battle, melting in his arms.

She knew she was heading for a massive heartache and pain, for what she was doing was not morally correct.

S whispered endearments promising to never hurt her and said she was like an intoxicant he could not seem to get out of his system, driving him mad with a passion only she could give respite to.

Serena could no longer deny her love and body to Samarthya and they fell back on the bed. S's body, a heavy sensual pleasure tingling every sensitive nerve ending of her body. They explored each other with a fevered hunger, their hands and lips frantically searching each other with an urgent intent that was going to lead to only one outcome.

In no time both of them were stripped of their clothes. Serena was at that moment tortured with what she was doing and at the same instance could not get away from this moment of forbidden love, which was exciting, and yet wrong. She did not want to think any more, just flow with the crimson tide of passion that was engulfing both of them.

S kissed every inch of her body driving her to a frenzy that needed a release, which only he could give.

"Serena you can tell me to stop now because after this I won't be able to hold my self back."

I looked at S through a cloud of sensual haze, understanding what an effort it was for him at that moment to give me a way out of this situation which was going to torture me with feelings of guilt.

At that moment I felt the strangest of emotions, I would not call love but something akin to a bonding that probably had been there, I thought bemusedly, from some time prior to this birth of mine!

I just pulled his face down and kissed him with a longing that gave him the answer to his question. From then on it was a journey of extreme pleasure. S was a wonderful lover, who had made me discover a new me that I did not know existed.

I was a wild wanton and uninhibited woman who was participating equally with her man giving him as much pleasure as he was giving her.

It was late night, Samarthya, my darling lover, had gone to sleep holding me, my head resting on his broad chest, his arms around my waist. I was wondering at the sudden turn my life had taken. Not so long ago, I had been a woman who had been grappling to find her life. And now, I had become this wanton woman who had made love to this handsome man, who till some days back had been an irritating stranger.

Slowly I realized that my feelings of guilt seemed to be disappearing. Being with, and loving S seemed to be the most natural and right thing for me. I think it was the darkness of the night, which obliterated or made light all the sins we humans commit, giving me the spurt of bravado that would vanish with the first ray of daylight.

I was still a married woman, albeit on the path to a separation and maybe a divorce. Could I dare to seek love which was forbidden and could I dare to dream of a future with this man to whom I had given my body and soul almost at the drop of a hat, to put it starkly.

But then, had he not made it clear in not so many words, that he was done loving and was not interested in a committed relationship.

Well at this time, I just wanted to live the moment not thinking about what and how this relationship would lead to or end up as. My emotions, I knew, were one sided.

I was shocked to realize that the thought of not seeing Samarthya squeezed my heart with an unbearable pain. I did not want to enter in a relationship, which was going to trap me. My life had been going around in an emotional circle, which I was trying to escape.

There were so many what if's, in my mind! What if S and his wife reconciled! Which as a good human being, I should feel happy for him because I was no home breaker.

I would be heartbroken losing him but at the same time happy that he could, unlike me, save his marriage and find happiness. What if he did not reciprocate the feelings of love I had for him. I mentally hit my self, saying it was rather late in the day to be thinking of that, for I had already given him my all, knowing well that at no point he had made any emotional commitments to me.

I also decided that I would tell Samarthya about my life. He had been so honest and candid about his marriage and life. If by any chance if this relationship progressed, I wanted him to know all about me and resolved that I would let him know my side of the story once we were in Cairo.

Finally exhausted, I went to sleep with feelings of happiness and contentment of being in my lover's arms.

CHAPTER 8

The next afternoon, we were taking the flight back to Cairo and this return journey was so much more intimate. We were lovers, comfortable with each other, I knew more about him than he knew about me. I loved him all the more for never asking me my side of the story, giving me space and time.

I was leaving the day after for Delhi, with S trying to get his flight preponed so that he could travel with me, but much to our dismay, the flight was fully booked. He could not get a ticket for the same, but there was an unsaid agreement that we were going to meet in Delhi.

We reached our Cairo hotel in the evening and were waiting at the reception for our respective keys. Our bodies comfortable and close to each other, we were very obviously a much in love couple to strangers. S had asked me to share his room with him but I had declined because I wanted some semblance of my own space though I knew that we would be spending the night together.

"Well, look who is here! My very own darling husband," came a drawling voice.

I stiffened and realized that Samarthya had tightened his arm holding me next to him.

It was Maheka, Samarthya's wife. What an extraordinarily beautiful woman! I just stood there totally frozen, staring at this vision of perfection. She was a tall slim woman, perfectly proportioned. She looked more like a movie star than a reputed journalist. Her peaches and milk complexion did not bear a single ravage of age, defying the truth that she was almost the same age as me, give or take a year or so. I felt like a dowdy old cow and inwardly cringed at the thought of hoping for a relationship with Samarthya, who had such a perfect woman as his wife.

Her hair was fashionably cut in a short bob that accentuated her beautiful jawline and her dark brown-eyes shone with a cynical amusement, when she saw the protective hand S had around my waist.

"Darling, another one of your conquests, though I must say, she is not your usual type," she spoke sotto voce lifting one perfectly arched winging brow.

She looked at me as one would at some poor creature that was not worth her attentions, turning to place a proprietorial hand on S, asking him with an amusing laugh whether she could share his room, thereby implying that I was sharing the room with him.

At that moment, I prided myself for having stuck to the decision of having my own room and just then the hotel reception called my name for handing over of my room key.

"Serena, I will be with you in some time," S finally spoke in that tension fraught moment.

But I just waived him off, and taking my room key, walked away from the scene with as much dignity as I could muster.

Maheka as a last warring retort had said,
"Serena, I am impressed! You have my husband totally enamored, normally his women are glamorous and young."

She had let me know that I was no match, and I too had been shocked to see her, and also ashamed to be seen as the other woman.

While entering the lift, much against my will, my eyes were drawn to S and his wife, who from a distance seemed to be engrossed in some discussion.

I walked like a zombie to my room, my mind totally blank of any emotions or thoughts.

Mechanically changing out of my travel clothes, I just went and stood under the stream of a cold shower, hoping I stayed in that numb and frozen state. I could not bear to think about Samarthya and the life story he had told me.

Had I been a stupid middle-aged woman who had got conned by a man in to believing she was some one special. His wife had mentioned that his normal women had been younger and beautiful and maybe I was an aberration that he was amusing himself with?

In view of today's happenings, all those stories of his wife and him having no relationship seemed to be having no credence. She seemed pretty used to his having girl friends and also had mentioned sharing his room, which did not corroborate with his story of them having no physical relationship.

I choked a cry of pain at having been made such a fool.

I don't know when evening had turned to night, the twinkling lights of Cairo as if celebrating my foolishness. I sat there in darkness wondering how and what my life would now lead to. It seemed like it was the second time in my life I was being hurt badly!

The ringing of the phone shook me out of my reverie. I knew it was Samarthya and let the phone ring. Finally, tired of the ringing, I just picked it up and kept it down, hoping that it would give him the message that I did not wish to speak to him.

But he was adamant, calling once again. This time I picked up the phone and could hear him calling out my name and I just kept the phone off the receiver.

After some time I heard a knock at the door, noticing with relief, it was the housekeeping staff with the bottled water that I had asked for. But my peace was short lived. A short while later, I heard Samarthya knock at my door, pleading with me to open the door and hear him out.

I stood on the other side of the door, my heart breaking with pain at his betrayal, and at the same time wanting to open the door and fly in to his arms and ask him to clarify and get all things back to what they had been between us.

But I knew it was not so easy, something had broken and I was not ready to mend it yet.

I stood on the other side of the door, with Samarthya aware that I was there, and despite his entreaties to open the door and hear him out, I refused to speak to him. Finally he left, saying that he would speak to me the next morning when I would be in a better frame of mind.

I was sleepless and decided to prepone my flight by a day because I could not bear to be in Cairo for even a minute longer. I called the Emirates call center and was fortunately able to get a ticket for the next day's flight. I quickly packed my bags and called the hotel reception informing them of my having to leave a day earlier. My flight was around twelve in the afternoon but I decided to leave the hotel early morning.

I had not slept the whole night, and at the crack of dawn, I showered and looked at my grief-ravaged face in the mirror. I promised myself never to let a man ever play with my emotions again. I was done with the species of men in general.

I informed my husband of coming a day earlier, as usual, he was not unduly concerned and for once I was relieved that I did not have to explain this sudden departure from Cairo.

The hotel taxi dropped me to the airport and after finishing my checking in formalities; I waited for my flight departure taking care to switch off my mobile phone.

The journey till Dubai seemed to last for an eternity and at the Dubai airport, when I switched on my mobile phone, there were some twenty missed calls from Samarthya and messages expressing his deep regret and anger at my having left in such a manner without having the courtesy of hearing his side of the story.

I was too immersed in my own grief, not wanting to hear his side of the story, letting my eyes believe what they had seen.

It had hurt me that day when Samarthya had not uttered a word in his wife's presence as if acknowledging her accusations.

On reaching Delhi, I had removed my international sim card and thrown it off in the bin, symbolically cutting the last link with Samarthya.

I just laughed cynically that it was my first holiday romance and that was all there was to it. The words of the poet Henry Wadsworth Longfellow came to my mind,

> "*Ships that pass in the night, and speak each other in passing*
> *Only a signal shown and a distant voice in the darkness*
> *So on the ocean of life we pass and speak one another*
> *Only a look and a voice, then darkness again and a silence.*"

CHAPTER 9

Three months had passed since I had come back from Cairo. I was going about my life like a machine. I was walking out of my hurt slowly, reflecting on which direction my personal life should take.

If nothing else, the affair with Samarthya Singh had woken me up from my own personal apathy and taught me a lesson that no man was worth my tears. I had to carve out my own destiny from now onwards.

I had gone on my journey of self-discovery, clinging with a hope deep in my heart, that I would some how revive my dying and stagnant marriage.

It was I, who had been emotionally pressurizing Jeh to give it another chance, and now there was a stark realization in my mind that it was a lost case or had been a lost case since a long time back.

My mind drifted back to the kaleidoscope of memories that I had thought of sharing with Samarthya, foolishly thinking that we had something deeper than just a holiday romance.

My earliest childhood memories had been of doting parents, who had me rather late in their lives and smothered me with their love and affection.

I was a pretty spoilt brat knowing very well that I could twist them around my tiny fingers.

My father was a middle level government employee in the Ministry of Urban Development.

We stayed in a compact government flat in a typical middle class housing block. We were content with an unassuming life having known no other. Fortunately, being the only child, my parents some how scrounged and sent me to a much better school than the other kids in the neighborhood. As a result, I was somewhat alienated from the other children, because most of them went to the local area school.

When I was in class seven, my father passed away suddenly, due to a massive heart attack. This was a tremendous shock to all, as he had been in perfect health, a simple man who lived frugally, never indulging in any worldly vices.

My mother, a typical housewife, had always been content to live in the shadow of her husband who had taken all the major decisions in life.

This sudden tragedy forced her to come out of her cocoon. Life had to go on, and we had to live and eat or eat and live, because that was all there was to life then.

My mother got a job in the Ministry on compassionate grounds. It was all very bewildering for her initially, but I give full kudos to her because she metamorphed into a woman with quiet strength, taking on the responsibility of looking after me seriously.

Fortunately, my father had been a sensible man and his insurance policies were able to take care of my educational needs. Had this not been the case, with the reduced salary, my mother would have had no recourse other than sending me to the local state school. So much for God's grace and mercies, Mother and me continued to plod on with life till I cleared my Class Ten exams with meritorious grades.

My mother wanted me to study the sciences and become an engineer or a doctor. I did not have an inclination for the sciences but secretly desired to study history and become an archaeologist and travel the world to study the ancient Mayan and Egyptian civilizations, which had fascinated me right from my grade eight, reading about them in the National Geographic magazine in the school library.

However I had come of an age, where I clearly understood that I did not have the luxury for such exotic inclinations. I would have to pursue an education that would make me employable and be a source of strength to my mother. She had valiantly taken on the task of giving me all that she could possibly provide, at times sacrificing things for herself, so that I would not miss out on an opportunity.

She had never forced me to do anything in life, so when the time came to give back some happiness to her, the least I could do was follow what she wanted me to study.

Those two years at school were the most frustrating ones in my life, because my heart was not in my science subjects. My dear mother, in retrospect, realized that I was not cut out to be a doctor or an engineer, but somehow I struggled and still managed to come through with decent grades.

By now I was clear that I would not seek a career in the sciences, and I was fortunate to get admission to study History in a Delhi University college. The next three years were the most exhilarating years of my life. I got to finally pursue a subject I loved, and decided that I would love to become a Teacher or a Professor depending on our monetary situation and my capabilities.

My mother was going to retire from her job in the next few years and both of us would not be able to survive on the pension she would receive.

My college was not coeducational. Having attended a convent school all my life, the mystery of the opposite sex was still unknown to me. This was strange, considering that during those days, girls were as clued in on boyfriends, as they are today. Now-a-days, girls are far more open about having a boyfriend and the sexual needs that they have, than our times when it was not so blatant. In a way, I appreciate the modern girl who knows her mind and what she wants, and is mostly able to manage her life.

I was a quiet girl, not given in to any fancy life style of fashionable clothes and outings.

One, I could not afford it, and secondly I also had no burning desire.

My head was firmly balanced on my shoulders, knowing well what I needed out of life.

Yes, there were some girls who met their material needs by having scores of boyfriends, who took care of them and their social needs, but I was clear that I was not one of them. I was not being judgmental because I realized each person had priorities in life, as long as it did not affect the others around them, It was their life and theirs to do what they wanted.

So fashion in college for me was my few sets of khadi printed kurtas and chooridars and my one bright purple mirror work kurta (yes my love with purple has sustained till date!) for some special occasion or when I needed an uplift of my mood. Yes I was a human too! Sometimes the monotony of living life got me also!

People who know me as Serena Khanna, who is in love with all things fashionable and has an impeccable taste for all things beautiful, would have been horrified and turned their noses at the mousy Serena Dev whose vocabulary was devoid of the word "fashion."

It was in college that I met my best friend Maya, who is till today, the only person I can pick up the phone and call any time of the day or night and know, without doubt that she is there for me. Maya's parents were fairly well off but never even once in my college life did she ever make me feel inferior. Our relationship was of equals.

There are very few people in life that we come across who exhibit such a wonderful sense of understanding and Maya was one of them.

Even in those early days of adulthood, she was as fine a human being as she is now and I had gravitated to her. I had initially thought she would not want me as her friend but how wrong I had been. Our friendship has withstood all tribulations of time, the biggest, her being Jeh's first cousin. She is the only person who knows all my fears; sorrows and the problems that my marriage with Jeh was going through, never letting her relationship with Jeh affect our friendship.

During college days, I used to do a lot of temporary jobs during vacations and sometimes part time jobs after college hours to help my mother monetarily. We had decided to buy a one bedroom flat as a home post her retirement. The monthly installments were proving to be a financial burden. We had no choice but to cope up with the financial stretch, as the home would have given my mother that feel of independence and security. She would always say that she did not want to burden me with her responsibility once I was married.

I would always, without fail, get annoyed and tell her that I would be looking after her whether I was married or not but yes she could still buy the flat for her own emotional security.

In the third year of my college, during the summer break, there was a major tourism fair and all the renowned travel and tourism companies were promoting their services. I was most keen to pick up a temporary job, since they were paying a pretty handsome remuneration for those fifteen days and to top this, the hostesses were allowed to keep the three sets of saris, which they would get to wear for those days. Also, the biggest attraction was the chance to secure a permanent job with one of the companies as soon as I was through with my college exams in the next few months.

I almost cried thinking of those days when such simple freebies as saris were such a lure and the money, which I had earned then, would not even buy one designer dress that I wore today.

But somehow the pleasures that I had achieved then, can never surpass having all the best things in life today.

Those days were so innocent and without any major expectations from life, no hurt, no pain, just living life in the moment.

Anyways, on a hot summer day I had donned one of my mother's saris for the first time. A beautiful navy blue check sari with a red border and fortunately, the blouse fitted with a few minor alterations done by her in anticipation of the interview the next day. The tourism fair had a compulsory dress code of a sari so there was no way I could have avoided wearing one.

My mother almost burst out crying, about how pretty I looked in a sari and that my kurtas did nothing for me as a girl. The whole day I tripped around practicing my walk in the sari and sandals, which were also a must, as this was a glamorous show, and I badly wanted to get this job.

I had never been so nervous in my life, and this opportunity seemed like it was a matter of life and death for me.

Ironically unknown to me, this was indeed a life-changing day for me. Little did I realize that I would be meeting my future husband, Jeh Khanna, and my life would take a complete turn!

My interview was scheduled in a central Delhi office at 11 a.m. But I was up early morning, my mind in tenterhooks. My mother had to reprimand me to stand still while she helped me tie the sari, as I was not yet an expert in the art of wearing one.

That day, I had taken the unaffordable luxury of an auto rickshaw, the inimitable mode of transport for most middle class Indians. I could not risk unraveling my sari; also I did not want to be late for my interview, waiting for the local bus service.

I reached the office well in time and there was a melee of beautiful girls dressed confidently in saris of the latest trends, waiting their turns for the interview.

I felt like a myna in a flock of jeweled macaws, my heart sinking with the thoughts of a prompt rejection. I must have been lost in my miserable thoughts and unknowingly my index finger nail was about to be the casualty when an amused male voice had remarked, "Are they tasty?"

I had literally jumped out of my seat on hearing the question, not sure whether it was addressed to me.

I looked up to see this very handsome young man, probably a few years older than me, wearing blue jeans and a check shirt and boat shoes, looking at me with an amused look in his eyes.

I was very embarrassed and immediately hid my hand in the folds of my sari.

"It's ok, I am just teasing you! Even I would chew my nails when I was tense and no amount of threats from my mother, of dipping my hands in vile liquids could get me to break this habit."

The good-looking young man went on talking much to my chagrin.

I looked sheepishly at him and nodded my head and he gave me a devastating smile. "Hey, relax it's just an interview, I am sure you will do well, and all the best!" and saying this he walked away.

That was my first meeting with Jeh, I had been so nervous and ill at ease that I had not even looked at him properly.

In our initial years of marriage Jeh had always teased me, saying that I had not even looked at him properly while he had seen me once and had been totally floored by the quiet little mouse, in a beautiful blue sari with a red border, who had sat eating her cheesy nail.

He had remembered everything about me that day, and now I think, with a lot of pain, where did all that love for me go. When did our relationship start going downhill to the point of no return? Where is my Jeh of those early heady days of our love?

When I was called for my interview, I had been flabbergasted to see the same handsome young man sitting in one corner of the large plush room. He had not acknowledged me and was totally engrossed in reading some thing. His presence in the room, and the comfortable and confident demeanor, let me know that he was some body important in the company.

The company's Human Resources Manager conducted the interview. He quizzed me on my strengths and weaknesses and asked whether I had travelled overseas and visited any countries.

I had never even travelled out of Delhi and told him so. My reply had him remark, then how would I be able to convince people to opt for the Companies' travel packages. I had glumly thought, well Serena, that's the end of your getting a job.

"Mr. Varma, you don't have to be a chef to be able to appreciate and eat good food," quipped the young man sitting in the corner of the room.

I had felt a surge of gratitude for his coming to my rescue, and had looked discreetly from my lowered eyes to see the Manager's reaction.

"Yes Mr. Khanna you are right! Ms. Dev seems to be otherwise quite a potential candidate for this job, but for this small drawback."

I had assured the Manager, my words more for the stranger who had rescued me from my pitfall, that I would do my best to read up and add to my knowledge. I would live up to their expectations if given a chance to work with the company.

The Manager had assured me that they would get back to me in a few days time as the fair was beginning from the following week.

I had left the office with mixed feelings, not knowing whether I would get the job for the summer, which would pave the way for a ready job for me as soon as my exams were over in a few months time.

My performance during the summer was critical for all this and I wanted this job desperately to take on the burden of helping my mother. I had already decided that I would enroll in a correspondence course for training as a schoolteacher and a long-term plan of studying later for my masters to enhance my teaching prospects.

In this life's plan, there was no place for romance or any other womanly desires, just this one burning quest to get this job.

The next day in college I had recounted to Maya my first serious interview for a potential job right after college. The short- term offer with the travel company for the summer would be the deciding factor for it.

She had asked me the name of the company and had not even given me a hint, that her uncle owned the company.

My happiness knew no bounds when I got a call from the travel agency that I and five other girls had got the summer job at the tourism fair.

In my heart I had resolved that I was going to work really hard and impress the Management into giving me the one permanent job that they were going to offer to the most deserving candidate. My mother felt I was being unnecessarily hyper, but I knew better that a history graduate without any additional qualifications would not get a decent well paying teaching job.

This job was in a reputed company and it was relatively well paying and would help me plan for my future academic endeavors also.

For the first time in my life, I had taken care to make sure that I looked attractive and wore my sari with care and ease, having practiced since the days after the interview as if, I was sure I would be selected for the job.

I knew that in this job, the outward appearance as well as my hard work and knowledge gained, would hold me in good stead.

I had reached the pavilion, a good one-hour before the fair started, to make sure that I did not bungle up on anything, though we had been given a brief one-day training.

I was bent over, zealously rereading the write-ups when I heard, "Hello, so you did clear the interview?"

I looked up to see the same young man nattily dressed in a beige linen suit, looking every inch a successful young entrepreneur.

I had stood up, stumbling a little due to my haste, because by now I had come to know he was Jeh Khanna, the son of the owner of the travel agency and had stuttered a good morning Sir to him.

Laughing, he told me not to Sir him, as he had yet to earn the respect and the success that came with the title, and address him by his name.

I had been embarrassed by his frank speech not knowing how to retort, because after all he was the owner's son. I had however mustered the courage and thanked him for helping me out of the tricky situation at the interview.

Jeh had very sweetly waived off my thanks, saying that I had deserved the job because of my own merit, and not because of a recommendation from his end. Then, with a tongue in cheek, had said that though his cousin Maya had made sure to let him know that you, Serena, were her best friend and teased me saying that her actual words had been, "my bestest friend."

"In light of such high recommendations and your own deserving capabilities, we had no choice but to make sure that you are here," said Jeh with a teasing look on his face.

I had been stunned to hear that Maya was his cousin. At that moment I could not have done anything but wait to get home. I wanted to blast her for not letting me know or at least fore warning me that he was her cousin.

Though I was desperate for a job, I wanted it on my own merits and not as a favor done to me because of my friendship with Maya.

The whole day had passed off in a whirl of activities, barely getting enough time to grab a sandwich and tea for lunch. I had not encountered Jeh Khanna after that and was secretly glad, because his presence would have reminded me that I was a recipient of a favor done by him and this was not sitting too well on my mind.

I had reached home by eight and called Maya right away. She had picked up my phone on the first ring as if she had been waiting for my call and before I could utter any word,

She had said, "Serena, before you fly off on your high horse, let me tell you that I had made sure from Jeh that you had got the job, and only later I had told him that you were my best friend!"

Maya knew me so well, she had anticipated my outburst and had been ready to sooth my ruffled feathers. She told me that no way would she have influenced Jeh, knowing how principled I was. She would not have upset our friendship for this, though stating a little later, wickedly, that had my chances been a little shaky, she would have tried bettering them.

"Serena, you never give me a chance where you could be indebted to me, please goof up sometime so that I can rescue you, my little mouse," said Maya lovingly.

I was blessed to have such a beautiful human being as my friend then, and even now she continues to be my closest friend.

CHAPTER 10

The next few days, I did not see Jeh at the pavilion and I was quite relieved, though Maya had reassured me that I had got the job on my own merit.

Some how, deep down, I had a feeling that if Jeh had not spoken up for me at the interview, even though the Manager had asked me a senseless question, I would not have been sitting here on the job.

A word of defense from the Boss man had helped me, I was sure about that. I did not want to think too much about it, wanting to prove to him that I was indeed capable and would not let him be disappointed for favoring me.

That day had been a very hectic one at the fair, with a more than the expected number of visitors. I had refused to go for a quick lunch break preferring to have cups of tea to keep me charged up. By the time we had wound up it was quite late, almost eight in the evening. While working, I had not paid heed, but it was later the realization hit me that it was late. I called my mother to let her know that I would be delayed, because taking the bus home and the wait would ensure that I would not be home before ten.

After packing up, I and another girl had reached the bus stop, which had a few other people also, so I was not unduly worried. I had been waiting for nearly thirty minutes, the other girl having already left, her bus having arrived, and then I was alone with a few men. I was a little jittery because they seemed to be staring at me or maybe I was imagining that in my nervousness.

In some more time I could feel the rush of panic set in and I looked desperately for an auto rickshaw, not bothering at the ill affordable astronomical fare, I would have to shell out. There were these very seedy looking men who had come to the bus stop and were positively eyeing me, making me feel extremely edgy.

An auto rickshaw stopped, but the driver refused, as he was going in the opposite direction and no amount of cajoling by me could stir him.

"Serena, is there a problem, can I help you?"

I had heard Jeh ask me that night and had almost turned in teary relief at seeing his familiar face.

I babbled incoherently about having got late, my bus not coming and there had been no other transport.

Jeh had gently steered me to his car parked at the bus stop side. He made me sit in the passenger seat asking me to relax. He offered me water, which I drank in a gulp, as if trying to wash away my fright and anxiety.

After that he offered to drive me home. I had some what recovered from my panicked state by then, and said I would be fine if he could just help me get an auto rickshaw and I could go home myself.

Jeh had just told me to shut up, because he had thought I was being hysterical, and asked me my address.

A little subdued by his scolding, I gave the directions to my home, in a middle class government-housing complex. I had never been conscious of Maya, who was a frequent visitor to our one bedroom home. We had done it up as aesthetically, in limited resources, as one could a drab government flat. Maya had always loved the food cooked by my mother, especially her rajma rice, the essential dish relished by all the Punjabis, people of the North Indian State of Punjab.

But today, I was conscious for the first time, of what Jeh would think of where I lived. This was a strange feeling considering that he barely knew me. The rest of the journey was completed in total silence. I kept squirming inwardly, that he must have been cursing his luck at having to help me, and to top that, of having offered to drop me.

On reaching my neighborhood I told him to drop me on the main road, as I did not want him to come inside on the narrow road leading to my building.

Jeh told me to stop wasting his time and to give him the directions to my flat, and soon enough we were in front of the shabby looking building. I quickly got down thanking him for the lift and the inconvenience I had caused him.

Jeh just smiled, as if aware that I wished him to be gone as soon as possible, but waited, as if to rile me till I had entered my building.

Much against my will I turned back to see if he was still there, and he was, and then with a quick wave, revved up the car engine and drove off. I stood there thinking about the ordeal I had undergone, and shuddered to think what would have happened if Jeh had not come by.

My mother on opening the door barraged me with questions on the lateness of the hour and how I had come. She was surprised to learn that Jeh Khanna had dropped me home. She did not at that moment ask me too many questions on the how and why of what had happened and the respect and love I had for her, went a few notches higher for her maturity, and the trust she had in me.

It was later in the night, I told her all about my ordeal and all she had said was, it was very kind of Jeh to help me out.

The next few days at the office were uneventful but I realized that for some reason Jeh was always around in the evening, busy working on his computer, and then one evening I had been slightly delayed and just before boarding my bus I noticed Jeh Khanna waiting in his car a little distance away. I was shocked and my heart was beating with an unknown emotion, I could not comprehend. I went and sat on the window seat and just then I saw Jeh pass by the bus and like a dramatic film scene, our eyes met for an instance and then he was gone.

It was a Sunday the next day and I was relieved that there was no office because I did not want to know or understand why Jeh had waited for me! Had he been doing it on the earlier days also and if so, why? My mind was in turmoil.

On Monday thankfully, Jeh was not around and just as I waited for my bus, his car came by and Jeh got out and almost ordered me to get in the car. I was very affronted at his high handedness but rather then creating a scene, which was being watched very avidly by my fellow commuters, I angrily got in the car.

"You may be the Boss of the company but that does not give you the right to order me around in my personal time," I almost pounced on Jeh.

He parked the car on the curbside and raised his hands in surrender and said that if he had asked me politely, nothing in the world would have induced me to get in, except the possibility of what had happened on that day when he happened to pass by.

"I don't want to even think about what could have happened to you Serena, had I not come by that day. Yes, after that, I have been watching out for you everyday and it was unfortunate that you saw me the other day," said Jeh.

"The answer to the question in your eyes, I don't know myself, why I feel this way for you!

All I know is that you bring out the protectiveness in me, you are like a small bedraggled puppy who needs to be cuddled and loved."

In that moment, I felt like a deflated balloon, I had no feelings and my body as if listless and floating in air. Jeh's words had hit me like a bolt of lightening. I, Serena Dev, had till date, never consciously thought of love, let alone having a boy friend.

I knew that love and boys were not for me and had never gone down that path. They would come but some time later in the foggy future, right now I had other priorities ruling my life.

"I am not a bedraggled puppy!" was all I could mutter to Jeh.

He had laughed and had pulled me in his arms and cried out, "Oh Serena, I think I love you, you are my brave princess who goes about slaying the demons all alone."

"Yes I love you, that's what I feel for you, I don't know when and how you came and entrapped me with your fierce independence. I want to protect you, fight the battles for you, be with you and look after you, my bedraggled puppy girl."

I was bombarded with an overdose of emotions, which had not been a part of my life, realizing with a start that I was still being held in the protective circle of Jeh's arms.

This was the first time I had been held by a man, and to my consternation, I liked the feeling. Then ashamed at my thoughts, I struggled to come out of them.

He had let go of me, telling me that he wanted to know more of me and no way was he going to let me get away from him.

Seeing the panic in my eyes, Jeh had gently patted my face and had said, "My silly baby, all I mean is, give me a chance to love you, and don't shut me out."

He had dropped me home, my mother at once realizing that some thing had changed in me. I had avoided her silent look of questioning. The next few days I was in total turmoil not knowing how to handle this avalanche of emotions. Love as an emotion had never been a part of my life, all my energies focused on charting a better future for my mother and myself. Then suddenly, love had laid its seed in my heart. It was unto me to let it emerge and grow or just remove it and go on with my uncomplicated life, the way it had been going on before Jeh came in my life.

The next few days at the exhibition had been very hectic leaving me no time to contemplate. Every evening Jeh would wait for me, to drop me home. We hardly spoke anything, he, as if understanding that I had been overwhelmed with what he had professed, needing time to think about it.

My mother though, had for the first time in my life, cautioned me, saying that I would end up hurt in this relationship. I guess I had become entangled in this new heady feeling of love and was not willing to give up so easily.

I had, slowly and surely, fallen in love with Jeh Khanna. In those rides back home, finally, I had let go of my complexes and accepted him for what he was, a considerate boy friend. It was very clear that he wanted me but he never forced himself on me.

He always maintained the distance, and some times I was secretly annoyed as to why he did not even want to kiss me. These newfound feelings of love were making me bold. I was quite tempted to take the initiative, one evening, I had like a loud mouth, asked him did he think I was desirable and did he not wish to kiss me once also?

Jeh had laughed, making me very annoyed, almost ready to pummel him when he had held both my hands and had said, "Wow, my hell cat! What a sea change, I am impressed!"

"I have been holding on to my urge to kiss you, but have held myself back, lest my straggly puppy bolted off."

Jeh had pulled me in his arms and gently kissed every inch of my face, almost worshipping it, then teased apart my lips, slowly kissing them.

For me, it had been a wondrous feeling of discovering what it was to love and be loved.

Now when I think back of that first kiss with Jeh and my first kiss with Samarthya, one had been all gentle and almost pristine and the other full of raging passion which had singed me to my core.

But then, I think I was not being fair. I had met Jeh when I was a young girl of not yet twenty, totally uninitiated to any passion.

I had been an anomaly for my times because girls my age had, even during those days, already been there and done that.

I laugh, and think that I had been fit to be admitted to a convent. Jeh had understood that and had been gentle with me.

Towards the last week of the exhibition, Jeh had asked me out for a dinner date and much to my annoyance, my mother had been very vociferous on the issue. She did not want me to go out with Jeh and to stop the friendship I was cultivating with him.

For the first time in my life I had told her that I was an adult, capable of taking my own decisions, whether they were good or bad. It was my problem and I was responsible for them. I had felt very bad on saying this, because my mother had always supported me in my life, and I had, by and large, agreed to all her decisions.

That was the last time my mother ever spoke on that subject, letting me do what I wanted to. It had been her way of showing her disapproval of the relationship I was having with Jeh.

I had tried assuring her that he was a very stable and mature young man for his age. He always treated me with love and care and no way he was going to take advantage of me, as she kept harping all the time.

Secretly I had wanted him to be more passionate, and I am sure my mother would have been horrified to know her darling daughter's thoughts!

The dinner date had me in tenterhooks, the whole day spent deliberating on what I should be wearing from my limited wardrobe, because no way could I afford to buy a new dress for my first date. Finally, I settled on a simple oyster pink georgette sari from my mother's wardrobe, which I teemed with her single strand of pearls. I thought I looked very pretty and elegant in the sari, hoping Jeh would be bowled over by me.

For the first time Jeh had come up to the flat to take me out and I was very nervous and a little embarrassed at the neat but shabby house that we kept.

He was very courteous to my mother, and in no time, had her comfortably talking to him as if she had known him from a long time. I gave him a small grateful smile, because he had known that my mother did not approve of him and despite that, he had taken pains to put her at ease. He had once again reinforced my belief in him, that he was a serious and a responsible man who loved me and would in no way ever hurt me.

Well how life changes! My Jeh of yester years was gone, lost in some dusty by lanes of my memory.

Jeh had taken me to a fancy uptown restaurant. All the young women were dressed in designer clothes and carrying handbags which probably would cost my whole year's earnings or more.

I had felt dowdy in my sari, deflated by the thought that Jeh must be cringing at my attire. He was such a darling, he put his arm around my waist, as if assuring me that I was the most beautiful woman in that place, and he was proud to be seen with me. At that instance, I think I had truly and madly fallen in love with Jeh Khanna and would have done anything for him.

That night, Jeh had me in a dizzy spell, with all the attention and love he professed for me. I don't recollect how the night went by so quickly, and as promised to my mother, he safely deposited me home by eleven in the night, an hour before the Cinderella time, lest I changed into a plain Jane who would lose her handsome prince.

Even after the exhibition was over, Jeh continued to date me. I had got over my hang-ups about how I looked and what I wore when I was with him. I was confident that he liked me for who I was and not where I lived or what outer skins I donned.

Just after my final year exams, Jeh asked me what I was planning to do next. I had laughingly told him that he was going to give me a permanent job, considering I had worked so hard that summer to land a job in his company.

"How about a permanent life time job of being my wife?" Jeh's remark had the effect of a bomb being dropped on me.

I sat there, my mouth open in surprise, and Jeh had very casually come and kissed me, hardly giving me any time to breath or think about what had been said, his kiss deepening with every second and passionately pulling me closer, his hands feverishly exploring my body.

Jeh had let go of his self –control, I could feel his aroused state of the body, and I had like a panicked buck, tried pulling out of his arms. But Jeh had held me tight and repeated his question, whether I wanted to be his wife.

At that moment all I could utter was a strangled yes, because I still could not believe that Jeh had proposed to me.

I had subconsciously avoided the question about what was to be the next level in our relationship. Would I just bask in this new feeling of love and attention from Jeh for some time and then go on with life as before? I had this fear deep down, that Jeh and I came from vastly different social backgrounds. It was one thing for him to have me as his girlfriend, but as a wife, would I fit in his social class of living?

I still could not believe, asking Jeh if he was sure of what he had said. He had laughed, saying I sure was a big dampener to his ardour and romantic mood. Here he was proposing to me to be his life partner, and I was being doubtful of his intentions.

I had told him that I considered myself as the luckiest girl at that moment, to have him think of having me as his life partner. My only fear, which he had reassured many a times in our relationship, was the vastly different social and economic background that I came from.

The fear that I would be a social embarrassment to him after some time, when the throes of love and passion had settled down, was all pervading.

He had told me that it was not I, but him, who was fortunate to have me as his life partner. He was attracted to my honesty and my quiet inner beauty. I was very unlike the girls he had known who were always trying to impress him with their glamorous looks.

"Jeh, are you marrying me because I am a plain Jane paragon of virtue?" I had laughingly asked him.

"No, you silly idiot, because I am madly in love with you and cannot think of a day without you anymore," saying this Jeh had pulled me back in his arms and kissed me dizzy till I had begged to be let go.

We had gone and given my mother the most pleasant shock of her life. The poor woman had gone all in a tizzy, wondering when and the how's of the wedding arrangements to be done. The Indian wedding ceremonies are an elaborate affair stretching on for days, with all the friends and family members that have to be invited.

She had questioned Jeh about his parents view, and it was then, that I came down with a slam to the ground. I could also see a look of concern and fear in my mother's eyes.

Jeh had not yet spoken to his parents about his plans to marry me, as they were out of the country. He was waiting for them to be back home, before breaking the news to them.

Seeing the look of concern, he had assured us that he was very clear that he was going to marry me, regardless of his parent's approval. However, he was sure his parents would welcome his choice of life partner with out any qualms.

How wrong he had been. Probably, this very resistance, of having me as their son's wife right from day one, had laid the seeds of our marriage heading for a breakdown.

Jeh's parents, Sudhir and Sunita Khanna, were the jet set darlings of the Delhi high society, who had envisaged an equally superior partner for their only darling son. It came as a big shock to them when he professed his love for an almost penniless girl from the wrong side of the town.

When pressures of disinheritance, and his mother's numerous melodramatic threats did not cut ice with Jeh, his parents finally gave in to their only son's demands and I was taken one evening to meet them.

I had been extremely nervous and was almost trembling with fear when I ventured in their stylish home in an up market part of Delhi.

Jeh had held my hand to give me the support and courage I badly needed, in the face of such adversity.

Jeh's mother was a typical high society fashion priestess, with all the right credentials and background to make her the undisputed queen of the social circles. She had the beauty and also the brains, using them effectively over the years to wage a silent and successful war against me. She had never overtly expressed any displeasure or said anything to me in front of Jeh, ensuring that he always thought his mother was right, and what ever she meant was for my own good. God, I was sick of hearing that statement!

Anyways, the meeting with his parents had been very awkward for me, with I, almost stammering in my replies, despite Jeh holding my hand to reassure me. I could, as a woman, recognize the discreet look of distaste cross my future mother-in law's face, as to what her son could see in me!

Jeh's father was a very cold man, not given to any expression of emotions, and I have still not figured out after so many years also, whether he has accepted me as a part of his son's life.

His life revolved around his business and the workings of his household was totally the domain of his wife, who ran it with unflinching precision.

That day, questions were asked about my parents and my life. Jeh's mother had stated that I had a lot to learn and catch up on, but that I need not worry. She had smiled her saccharine sweet smile, which over the years I have come to hate, and had said, she would gladly help me understand the social mores and etiquettes of the society in which they lived.

"Darling, you will not survive a day, if you don't walk and talk the society we live in. Of course, only if you want my help, because I would not have my darling Jeh face any embarrassment!" she had coolly drawled, reminding me of the vast chasm that existed between them and me.

Jeh to my relief had protested that I was not a moron and would not shame him or the family, and I would always appreciate and take his mother's advice as and when I needed it.

On the way back I had been very quiet, my morale had been very low. At one point, I had almost burst in to tears, telling Jeh to forget about marrying me, because I was sure I would not fit in with his social background and be a cause of embarrassment to him.

He had gathered me in his arms assuring me that I was marrying him and not his society. He was lucky that I was going to be his wife and to never feel in any way that I was inferior to the fake and pretentious women who floated in the society circles.

In our Indian culture, marriages are not only the joining of two people but also the accompanying families. Their getting along is also crucial to the marriage being a success. Considering Jeh's parent's opinion about me and my mother, I still had a lot of doubts but somehow Jeh's love and assurances overrode all.

CHAPTER 11

It was early December, when Jeh and I got married. There had been many rounds of discussions on the wedding ceremonies, and I had looked upon my mother with great pride, because in spite of the many subtle and not so subtle barbs by Jeh's mother about our financial status, she had maintained her dignity.

They had offered to take care of all the wedding expenses, which she had declined, and the wedding took place in an Army club which had been arranged by my mother's cousin. Of course, we could not have entertained the sheer number of guests from Jeh's side, so only the closest of friends and relatives had been invited, much to the displeasure of his parents.

A party hosted by my in-laws, which had been the talk of the town for months, had followed the wedding. The who's who of the social and political circles of Delhi had graced the party.

It had been a bewildering experience for me to be thrown from anonymity to the center stage of the Delhi society.

Some of them had been very generous in welcoming me, while others had a look in their eyes, as to how I had managed to snare the most eligible man in the society. That day, and the succeeding few days before we left for our honeymoon to Seychelles, had been a flurry of parties and more parties.

I had been relieved to get away from all that attention and the next fifteen days had been the most idyllic and romantic time of my life.

We had stayed at an exotic and luxurious resort, and for the first few days we had barely stepped out of the room, lost in the heady pursuits of lovemaking and discovering each other.

Jeh had been a considerate and tender lover and my journey into womanhood was a pleasurable one. I, who had never ever seen a man intimately, had, from a puritan, become a woman enraptured with the pleasures of lovemaking. Jeh and I could not seem to have enough of each other, and every day was a different discovery of our selves, and we were inseparable.

We came back to Delhi, and though we had a separate apartment in the palatial house, my mother- in- law ruled my life, and has continued to do so till today. She has cleverly made the rift in our marriage grow wider and wider, to the point, where it can no longer be bridged with any positivity.

A few months after my marriage, I met Sonya Singh, the daughter of the business partner in the family's travel firm. She had come back from the States after completing her management degree and a welcome party was being organized for her. I had never seen my mother-in-law in such an excited frenzy, the whole house was being turned upside down, guest lists were being drawn and the food menus being planned with great deliberations.

It had seemed odd to me at that time, wondering what was so special about Sonya, who was driving my otherwise cool mother-in-law to such an excited flurry. I had incidentally asked Jeh about her and he had just laughed it off saying that mother had a soft spot for her. It was then I realized the extent of the soft spot, for I was no fool!

Sonya and Jeh had practically grown up together, having attended the same prestigious school favored by the elite and the rich of the Delhi society. She was two years his junior and she had followed him to the States for completing her higher education. I was told by many, that Jeh and Sonya had been the life of parties and were a popular couple who were seen together at all the society do's.

In the coming months, I was given enough hints by gossip mongering bitchy women, that it had been a fore gone conclusion that the Khanna's and the Singh's were going to cement the business relationship to a more lasting one with the expected marriage of their children. I could now understand the veiled hostility of my in-laws; I had upset the apple cart, and to top it, had nothing in credit, except an almost penniless heritage when compared to theirs.

But it was Jeh's attraction and his marrying me instead of Sonya, that still puzzled me, and deep down, I had yet to overcome the insecurity and my belief in his love for me.

I met Sonya at the welcome home party hosted by my in-laws, and it had been hate at first sight, for both of us.

She was like an exotic hot -house orchid with flawless complexion of a porcelain doll, pouty red lips, with jet -black hair. Her mother was a French woman, who had come on a travel holiday to India, and had fallen in love and married and settled in Delhi.

The moment I had walked in to the room with Jeh, there had been a lull in the conversations, and everyone had waited to see the encounter we two would have. Some had shown an obscene openness and others had acted nonchalant, but all had wanted to see how Sonya would react to me.

She had launched herself at Jeh, flinging herself at him and crying out how she had missed him in the last six months, and how could he have got married without waiting for her.

Then she had looked at me, her bluish green eyes cold and glittering, as if sizing up an adversary, and said with a petulant voice, "So, you are the girl who has stolen my dearest friend?"

I wanted to retort that I had not stolen her dearest friend, that he had swept me off my feet, and thus take away the possessive look in Sonya's eyes.

Since I did not want to give fodder to the eager ears and eyes as they were trained in our direction, I had simply smiled and said, "He is still your friend."

The relationship with Sonya had started on a back foot. She always took digs at my looks and attire and the supposed lack of my etiquettes at any social events where we met, and to top it, my mother-in-law seemed to encourage her. They both have been successful, because Sonya is finally back in Jeh's life, and my mother-in-law, even after all these years, has never accepted me as a part of the family and now goes about with a look of a victor in her eyes!

Well, good for all of them, because I have finally moved on, at least one thing this holiday has made me realize, that I no longer love Jeh and have been clinging to a relationship that has been dead for long.

The Jeh I had met and fallen in love with was no longer the same man. I guess it happens only in story -books, handsome and rich hero falling for the poor and simple heroine and living happily ever after!

In the real world things are more complicated and just love cannot conquer all. I guess I am being cynical, but now I want to feel and be what I want to be. I have had enough of living my life according to the expectations of others.

Some how, I don't blame only Jeh for the breakup of our marriage. I am also partly responsible for it. In all these years I changed from the simple girl that he had fallen for, to a woman constantly struggling to become a sophisticated fashionable woman like the Sonya's of the society.

I was fearful that if I did not reinvent myself from the plain jane Serena, I would lose Jeh. I did lose him because in my constant insecurities to be the Serena Khanna of today, I had pushed Jeh away from me.

He could never understand my insecurities, for he had grown up in a lap of luxury and the social mores I was trying to ape were a natural way of life for him. All this took a toll. Though I had become the Serena Khanna of today, I had lost being my own natural self.

My first pregnancy, a year and half after our marriage, did not go too well with my mother-in-law, as she thought it was too early in our marriage to become parents, and was pretty implicit in stating that I was being very middle class.

This was not the only reason why she had been very anti my having a child so soon; a major well-guarded family secret had tumbled out when Jeh had confided in me the reason for his mother's hostility.

Apparently my father-in-law, whose nonchalant do-not-bother-me attitude I can now understand, had, as a young man fallen madly in love with a beautiful young refugee girl whose family had relocated to Delhi from then unpartitioned Punjab.

Unfortunately like me, she too did not have any wealth or the social standing to match the illustrious family of Diwan Devi Dayal Khanna. He offered the girl and her family a sizeable amount of money to end her relationship with his only son Sudhir, a la melodramatic old time Hindi movies.

But the matter had escalated far more than that. Apparently, she was pregnant and during those days, it was matter of great shame, not only for her family, but also would have caused a major scandal in the Delhi society.

Tragically my father-in-law, unlike Jeh, had capitulated to his father's threats and refused to acknowledge that the child was his.

The poor girl and her family had no recourse, but to accept the money and leave Delhi to relocate to some other city, to hold on to what ever was left of their pride.

My father-in-law was promptly married off to a girl from a rich and prominent business family of Punjab, who brought a lot of additional wealth and stature to add to the Khanna family name.

A few months after my father-in-law's marriage, a message had come from an obscure town in the hinterlands of Punjab that the unfortunate girl, jilted by Jeh's father, had died giving birth to a girl child.

I am sure she must have died of a heart-break, for putting her faith and loving a man who had dealt her such a cruel fate.

Finally he must have suffered guilt feelings, knowing that the child was his, because he had fought with his father, threatening to walk away from the marriage, if the child was not adopted in the family.

In all this drama, my mother-in-law had felt very bitter and cheated. During those days, it would have been an insult for her family honor if the marriage broke up within a few months, and her own life ruined. As a result she had swallowed a bitter pill and continued with the marriage.

However, she had vehemently put her foot down, that under no circumstances would she allow the girl to be brought up in her home, and once again Jeh's father had fallen in with his family and wife's demands, and the girl was adopted by some distant widowed aunt.

She was brought up with all the care and comforts but with out ever having the Khanna name to her credit.

My mother-in-law, rightly so, had not taken kindly to this, as no woman likes to be cheated by her man, and had always been very bitter and hostile towards Jeh's half sister.

But I felt her hostility towards the child was unfair, because it was not the poor and innocent child's fault that her father had not stood up and married the woman he had loved.

So in all those years, Jeh's half sister Aditi, had been treated like a forbidden entity, never to be spoken of, but for the occasional fights that still happened between his parents else Jeh would have never known of her existence.

Of course, Aditi had never known that she had a father and also a half brother. Both Jeh and I felt, it was kinder and better that way, than for her to know that her father had deserted her mother and had even refused to acknowledge her as his child at one point.

Some things in life are better left as secrets, because opening a Pandora's box can only bring more pain and grief to all the concerned parties.

So Aditi just knew of Jeh's father as an indulgent uncle and Jeh as a cousin brother who was very caring and lavish, making sure that she never lacked anything in life.

I loved Jeh for his sensitivity in having accepted Aditi and not being bitter with her, like his mother.

Aditi had got married a few years prior to our marriage, and had emigrated to Australia, much to his mother relief, who had always disliked her husband, and later, Jeh's visits to meet Aditi.

I had met Aditi much later in our marriage, when we had gone to Australia for a holiday and had spent a few days with her and found her to be a lovely girl, and it had seemed a pity that Jeh could not acknowledge her as his sister.

We had kept in touch over the years intermittently and then I had got busy with my own life and the ensuing problems that came with it.

So despite my mother-in-law's displeasure, Jeh and I, had been delighted with the birth of our first son, and had fallen into the role of parents with ease and pride.

And two years later, I had my second son. We had been desperately hoping for a girl to complete our happy family, but that was not to be and much as I would have liked to try and have a daughter, Jeh did not want another child.

My mother-in-law had harbored hopes that maybe Jeh would get over his infatuation, as she said, over me, and our marriage could have ended easily, if there were no children involved. I had, at that time, dashed all her aspirations by having two sons.

Anyway, her precious Jeh was free! I was soon going to be out of his life.

Fortunately for me, my sons did not have to bear the leper treatment, for after all, they were the Khanna bloodline! According to my mother-in-law there was something at least I had done right, by giving the family their successors. I don't understand this timeless silly notion of sons being the heirs of the family name because girls are more loving and responsible towards their parents.

Sonya had realized, by now, that her chances of being Jeh's wife were a distant possibility and had, after a few years, married a wealthy business- man in the States and had left India.

That was the best thing that had happened for me. The years that she had been away, I managed to find a place for myself in the society. Earlier the women had been greatly influenced by her constant bitching and running-me-down tirades.

I now reflect, with shame, as to how I could have become so needy and unsure that I needed the acceptance of these fake and conceited women for my self worth. Anyways it was better late than never. I was going to make sure that I would never have to depend on anyone for my emotional well- being.

So life during those years was honky dory, there was also a sort of truce from my mother-in-law, who let me know that I was doing good as far as my clothes sense and society etiquettes were concerned, pompously stating, "After all living in a good society and having money helps!"

I wanted to tell her that, many in the said society had an atrocious dress sense and abominable manners which money had not refined.

However, like always, I avoided confrontations that made life miserable, and took the more easy way of acceptance and in the process slowly becoming like a doormat, on which every one could tread upon.

There were happier times also when I would travel with Jeh on his business meets and for some time I could forget the responsibility of being a mother and a daughter-in-law.

Those were the times when I did not have to be someone else, just the Serena, Jeh had fallen in love with.

All those travels widened my horizons. I learnt a lot about varied cultural heritages, and had one day expressed a desire, if I could come back to work at the family business. Jeh had been non- committal, stating that our children were still young and needed more time, and I could always come back to work after they were grown up.

He had suggested that I should join his mother in the various charities she was involved in. Thus, all my aspirations to do something besides looking after my home and children, were dashed since I did not have any burning desire to do charities with his mother, which were more a means of remaining in the society headlines, than any real worthwhile contributions by her.

But my relatively good period of matrimonial harmony did not last for long. Sonya, like a boomerang, bounced back in to our lives.

Her decade old marriage, sans any children, had not worked. I bitchily thought, it was no wonder, because which man could have tolerated a selfish and vain woman for that long, and her husband must have been a saint, having borne her for so long.

Sonya slipped back into the society circles with her accustomed ease, and in no time she was back to being the prima donna. Her earlier blatant antagonism was now couched. In front of Jeh, she would project a very friendly attitude towards me, and would show him how much she valued us, by bringing presents for the boys and myself.

All this would be shown with great show, in front of Jeh, and my mother-in-law would gush over her generosity and admire Sonya's impeccable tastes in clothes and all things that she did.

Sonya also very cleverly projected her self as the frail and wronged woman, who had been dealt an undeserved blow by life. She was successful in this, because she had Jeh's sympathies, and on rare occasions when I had expressed that one should see a coin from both sides, Jeh had been very defensive for Sonya.

He and his mother were totally taken in by her clever wiles, and in the end I would end up looking like a nasty unsympathetic woman, who was jealous of a woman who was being so good to me.

These lead to the first serious fights I had with Jeh over Sonya, I tried telling him that her behavior towards me was a façade; in actual she was trying to break our marriage by creating a rift between the two of us. Jeh always counteracted that it was my imagination and my bias towards her that was making me miserable and insecure, and that I should grow up and accept Sonya as his good friend and nothing more.

I did not know how to get across to Jeh that Sonya was not what she portrayed to him, and thus everyday led to my hurt deepening, that my husband and life partner did not believe in me.

Sonya's father decided to retire from active business and Jeh offered to buy out their share of the business.

This was the start of serious troubles in my marriage, for Sonya decided to become an active partner and started going to the office and running the day-to-day business of the firm.

Now, she had Jeh practically the whole day with her, and also started travelling with him on outdoor locations for conferences and meetings.

I started to become an emotional wreck, constantly edgy about the relationship and the growing comfort that Jeh seemed to have with Sonya. Logically, when I reasoned with myself, I knew that he had known Sonya since childhood and the comfort level was but natural. It was just my woman's intuition, and also the scheming of my mother in law and Sonya's damsel in distress act, that was tormenting me to no end.

Every day of our life had become a torture. Fortunately both the boys were in a boarding school, and were not witness to our constant fights and my insecurities, which were slowly driving us apart.

Then some thing changed drastically in our relationship!

Jeh and Sonya were going for ten days to Paris for a tourism event. Jeh had offered to take me with him, though they would have been busy with conferences and meetings. He had said I could go see Paris myself during the day, and later at night, we could enjoy the nightlife that the most romantic city of the world offered, or alternatively I could join him after the conference was over, and we could have the much needed bonding that we had been lacking.

He had said we could sit down and figure out what was going wrong with our marriage, and work at it. I had agreed to come later on, as I could not bear to be with Sonya, who would have been there, for Jeh would have surely invited her for the outings.

I had flown to Paris later, not wanting Sonya anywhere near us, especially since we had to figure out how to stop our marriage from breaking apart.

Jeh had hired a rental car for the duration of his stay in Paris, and came to pick me up from the airport. He had seen me as soon as I came out of the terminal and after a quick kiss and a hug helped me stow my suitcases in the car boot, and just as I turned to open the car door, I saw Sonya already sitting on the front seat. She made some polite murmuring of asking if I would like to sit with Jeh in the front and catch up with him, as both of us had been apart.

My mood had deflated; all my happiness vanished in an instant when I saw the smug look of a cat that had captured her prey. I knew, in that instance, that her equation with Jeh had changed in some way.

I had pulled my self together, with super human effort, keeping a normal tone, had told her not to be silly, and that I could sit at the back. I had enough time to catch up with Jeh, it was not as if we had been apart for years, just a mere ten days.

During the ride back, Sonya had very cleverly let me know, that the last ten days had been the best days of her life, adding with a studied pause, about learning so much about the business, going out for dinners, and meeting interesting people. She would deliberately name some so and so who had been witty, and then related an incident about some Texan oil millionaire who had been coming down heavily on her, and how Jeh had come at the opportune moment and rescued her.

Then turning towards Jeh, had laid her hand on his arm, and simpered how grateful she was to him and what a wonderful friend he was.

Men are so idiotic; I don't understand how they cannot look through the clever manipulations of women like Sonya's of the world. I could see the satisfied look on Jeh's face on being flattered by Sonya.

Soon, we had reached the hotel where Jeh and Sonya were staying. She was leaving in the evening and turning towards me with a very woebegone look said to me, "Serena, I don't want Jeh to be away from you for one moment also, I can understand how difficult it must be for you, when Jeh and I have to go away for our business commitments," and turning to Jeh said, "I will leave for the airport myself."

The bitch that she was, in those words, she let me know how I must be tortured by her proximity to my husband, and at the same time, showing Jeh how she was concerned for me. Jeh at once assured her that she did not have to take a taxi, that he and I will go drop her to the airport.

We both had looked at each other, and understood very well what message she had conveyed to me, but to continue with her charade, I had to force myself and tell her that I understood that both she and Jeh had to work and he could not be with me all the times.

Later on, during lunch, in her conversations, she let me know, how she had dragged Jeh to the designer boutiques and bought loads of clothes.

"Serena Darling, you know my passion and taste for clothes! I can recommend some of the design houses who will gladly help you figure out what is the best for you, especially if you give them my reference."

"Poor Jeh, I really bugged him, but he was sweet enough to sit through my trial dress sessions, and also helped me choose them."

I could feel myself go cold with each word she was uttering, and could barely swallow the food that seemed tasteless, feeling I would choke on it if I had another bite.

I pleaded a splitting headache due to the journey, and excused myself, leaving Jeh and Sonya to continue with the lunch. Later on, when Jeh came to the room I pretended to be asleep, because I knew I would not be able to control myself and we would have had a massive row.

Jeh continued to be in the room, working on his laptop, and I finally gave in to emotional exhaustion and went to sleep. Later in the evening, Jeh woke me up; he had made a cup of tea for me, and asked me how I was feeling. Not wanting to go to the airport, I had lied saying I was still a little groggy with the headache, and would he mind, if I did not come along.

He had assured me it was perfectly all right for me to rest, while he went to drop Sonya to the airport.

That night, I was still miserable, and after dinner Jeh had asked me why I was so off mood and then had started our fight, which was the start of the end of our life together.

I had confronted Jeh on his relationship with Sonya, I threw back Sonya's words at him, how he had helped choose her outfits, and the time he had been spending with her. Words had flown thick and fast between us, my sixth sense warning me that things had changed between Sonya and Jeh. I had asked him to tell me the truth of their relationship so that I could be at peace. I asked if he had a physical relationship with Sonya, because her body language had told me that she had that physical comfort with him that only lovers could have had. My question, and the guilty look on Jeh's face, told me all.

I needed no answer, and my whole world spun and shattered with that revelation. I sat there like a zombie, uncomprehending, Jeh's voice coming to me as if from a long tunnel.

That was when I least expected; Jeh dropped another bomb on me, saying that he needed time to rethink our relationship. Maybe it was best if we separated for some time and gave each other time to reflect on what was going wrong and save the marriage.

I felt like a tree that had been struck by lightening, twice, all burnt and dead.

How did that night pass by, I still do not recall. All I remember was curling up like a miserable ball on the sofa, looking out at the twinkling lights of the Paris skyline and the iconic Eiffel tower through the French windows. My silent tears kept pouring refusing to dry up, as if wanting to wash away the hurt.

Some time during the night, Jeh had asked me to come and lie down on the bed, but I had looked at it, wondering if he had made love to Sonya on it and curling with distaste, I had ignored his request.

There was now no question of my staying back in Paris for the next three days, but some pigheaded pride of not giving Sonya the pleasure of having routed me, made me ask Jeh to book a separate room for me. He had objected to this, but finally gave in, when he realized I was in no mood to comply.

Paris evokes feelings of love and romance, but for me it was the death of my love, my being, as a woman of some worth.

I could not get my self to venture out of the room to see what the city had to offer, and barely ate anything, waiting for the day when I could board the flight back to Delhi.

On the long flight back home, I had barely spoken to Jeh, just the necessary monosyllabic answers.

I was still raw and hurting badly, to sit down and talk with him about what next in our lives.

Once back in Delhi, Jeh and I finally had our talks without any melodramas from my end. We decided that we would maintain a false charade of our marriage, for a few more months, as our younger son was leaving for the States for his higher education and then take a separation. Our elder son was already studying in a New York college. It would come as a shock to them, as they had never seen us ever fight.

It was just a matter of few months, and after that, I would shift out of the family home into an apartment that we already owned.

Jeh had assured me, that during this period, I would have no financial constraints and he would arrange to deposit a more than adequate monthly sum in to my bank account.

Did he think money could have bought me all the happiness and solved the problems that we were having? Well, at least I did not have to worry about my every day living expenses.

I had over the years become pragmatic, having grown up in an atmosphere where financial security had been the main issue.

This was not the only blow that life would be giving me; there was another whammy in store for me.

I had gone over to meet my mother to break the news to her that I would be in a separation period with my husband till we could decide if we wanted to divorce. I wanted her to come and stay with me and that is when she revealed that she had been diagnosed with breast cancer, which was in the last stages.

I was devastated to hear the news, and also learn that she had a limited time, despite my pleadings that we would seek the best treatment for her, she had refused saying it was of no use, and would rather spend her balance time with me than on hospital beds.

I had shared this with Jeh, and he had been very supportive and had tried convincing mother to opt for treatment overseas, but it was to no avail. Finally after a few months, my son left for his college and I shifted to the apartment along with my mother.

In all these trying times, the look of pleasure on my mother in law's face was obscene. One would think that after twenty years, she would have accepted me and discouraged us from separating, but I guess I was in a worse position than the family dog, Brutus, who was the beneficiary of her affections.

I was sad parting with him, because I had come to truly love the adorable mutt, who had been a mute spectator to my grief.

Mother had lived for barely four months after we had shifted to the apartment. I had done everything possible to make her comfortable, but cancer had snatched my only source of strength, and the period after that had been extremely traumatic for me.

I had kept my sons away from the trauma I had been facing because there was no point making them choose loyalties.

It was the friendship of Maya that had pulled me through the stressful period. She had practically taken control of my life as I had literally given up on it, my self-confidence at rock bottom, with me swimming in an ocean of self- pity, just about ready to sink and drown.

I had never been bone thin, and all these months of stress had taken a toll. I was overweight by almost ten kilos, my hair in a disreputable state, and my face was all puffy and sickly.

The Serena of a year back, despite the turmoil, would have been horrified to see this woman. When I saw myself in the mirror, I was ashamed of myself, and at that moment decided that I have to be back and take control of my life. One man could not hold the key to my happiness, and I was going to search for me.

The first thing Maya had done, was to sign me up for a gym membership, and then dragged me to the upmarket salon, which I frequented.

The French hairdresser had lamented the state of my beautiful hair, chiding me for getting them in such a mess, and then spent painstaking hours getting my mane to its former glory.

With a new flattering cut and color, and a wonderful day at the spa, I was ready to take on the world once again.

Well, at least, Jeh's generous allowance allowed me these luxuries, and for once I had no qualms spending his money.

The next couple of months, I was a woman on a mission. I hit the gym, sometimes twice in a day, and had healthy meals, and almost knocked off the excess baggage I had accumulated on my self. I wished the hurt, which was festering like a bad wound, could also go away as easily.

I was working towards it and knew it would take me some time but I would come out of it.

Looking in the mirror, I saw a middle aged woman, who looked pretty okay for her age.

I had got rid of the external ravages, and that's when I had hit upon the idea of a solo holiday, to find my self-confidence and me. What better place then Egypt, the land of the pyramids, and my fascination since school days? For some reason Jeh and I had still not visited Egypt and in retrospect I think it was fated to be so.

CHAPTER 12

I stood looking out of the living room window. Winter had been exceptionally cold this time in Delhi. The orange street-light struggled to shine thru the fog, which like a creature, was slowly devouring all in its path. It had been almost six months since I ran away from Cairo. I wish my memories of Samarthya, and the passion we shared, would become blurred as the dense fog outside.

I had gone to Egypt thinking that I was going to find my self-confidence, and a hope, that Jeh and I would give our marriage another chance.

But fate had decried something else, with Samarthya stepping in my life. He had made me realize I was no longer in love with Jeh, because I had given my body and soul to an almost stranger.

Much as my mind denied, it had been love at first sight for me. I still loved Samarthya with a painful intensity, despite my belief that he had been dishonest with me about the relationship he shared with his wife, Maheka.

I seemed to have bad luck as far as love was concerned. Though hurting badly, this time I had not allowed myself to wallow in self-pity, and make a mess of myself. I guess I was improving with each setback in love, laughing cynically, maybe third time lucky.

I knew I would never lay myself open to hurt again; S had made a big dent in my heart. Many times I had been tempted to call on the numbers from the visiting card he had given me, because I knew he was in Delhi.

I wondered if he thought of me and missed me as much as I did. Had he ever tried finding me, because he did not have my phone numbers or knew where I was staying? All these questions sometimes really troubled me. I would shake my self out of the misery by reminding myself that if he wanted, he could have easily found out, because I had mentioned to him the name of our travel company. Then, sometimes, I would give him benefit of doubt, that he may have forgotten it.

One thing had become clear to me; I had asked Jeh for a divorce, and for some moments, I had been hurt at how easily he had agreed to it.

He was, as if relieved, that I was not going to contest, and plead with him to save our marriage. Due to some stupid womanly pride, I had wanted to tell him that I too had discovered passion and love, but some thing had held me back. What was the point in crowing about it, when it was already gone and lost?

But, somehow, I was also more sympathetic and understanding, knowing how it felt to be separated from some one you love.

Jeh and I, much to the distress of our sons, divorced by mutual consent. It was better in the long run for them, because I am sure, the bitterness of our marriage would have spilt out in the open, and eventually affected them too. I did not want them to make choices and be pulled in the opposite directions, because they loved both of us equally.

Jeh had been extremely generous. He had made sure, I need not have worked ever to support myself. It may sound strange, but we are more comfortable with each other now. I call him sometimes, when I am not clear about certain investments and tax issues.

Jeh and Sonya are engaged now, and she is reveling in the society parties, finally with Jeh at her side. I am no longer interested in attending these parties, not because of her or that people may look at me with pitying eyes, but because I have realized I was never a part of them. It sort of makes me feel liberated that I no longer have to enact charades.

Today, while switching television channels, I accidentally saw Samarthya interviewing a prominent Middle East ruler. My heart stopped beating for a second. I just sat there, fixed, seeing the familiar heart breaking good looks, and the amused cynical lift of his left eyebrow. All I could hear was the deep sexy baritone voice and had no clue of what was being said by him. His hair seemed a little longer and his face looked thinner.

I almost reached out to touch him on the television screen, and then jolted out of my dream.

"Hell, Serena, You cannot go down that path again!" I silently screamed at myself. I had almost learnt to curb the pain in my heart, and had decided I would go away for the next six months to be with my elder son in the States. I was contemplating to study further, a desire that had been put on the back burner, after I got married.

Now, I had the time and the resources, and it was best for me to go away from Delhi. I knew, one day, I would take the courage and call Samarthya, and once again walk the path of destruction.

The best thing for me would be to get away from the temptation, which was waiting for me to fall.

That night, I dreamt of Samarthya and me making passionate love, and it felt almost real, my hands reaching out, imploring him to take me.

Samarthya had engulfed me in his arms, we were both furiously kissing each other like two thirsty people who had found water and could not seem to have enough of it.

His lips exploring every inch of my naked fevered body. My fingers curled in the silver streaked hair, which I always thought were very sexy, almost painfully pulling his head down, begging him to plunder my mouth.

I had cried out his name in my sleep, begging him to take me, and to relieve me of the painful torture that plagued my body.

It was then I woke up, and realized with excruciating agony, that it was a dream. I could not sleep anymore. My mind was in turmoil, wanting to call Samarthya, and putting an end to this misery.

It would become clear if he wanted me, or else I would once again pick up the broken pieces of my heart, and embark on my new path of life.

But somehow, I could not gather the courage to call him now, or later. Like a silly fool, I wanted to live with the hope that he wanted me, but did not know my whereabouts. This was better than facing the harsh reality of a rejection.

My tortured mind expressing my deep love for Samarthya, in words that came out from my very core!

> I am because you are
> Without you my love
> I am like the shifting sands of the desert
> That has no shores
> A touch of your glance
> And I burn in the fires of your passion
> Only You and only You
> Make me come alive
> With the touch of your lips on my
> fevered skin
> Every day becomes an inspiration
> When we duel with our minds
> Without you my love
> I am nothing
> But an empty shell
> Rolling aimlessly on the sands of time.

In that miserable night, I resolved that I would, in earnest plan my new life, and leave the past behind. I did not want to stay with my sons, who had their own lives. I wanted a life, which was unencumbered with any expectations, either mine towards my sons or vice versa.

It was strange, how easy and comfortable I felt calling Jeh, and asking his advice on where and how I could rent an apartment in New York.

A weight had been lifted off from our relationship, and we seemed to be getting along quite well.

Jeh had insisted on a one- bedroom apartment in an upmarket area of Manhattan, insisting that his wife could not stay in anything less, and for a moment there was a stunned silence at what had been said.

I had laughed and diffused the embarrassing situation by telling him, "You better get used to Serena Dev, Mr Jeh Khanna." I had reverted to my maiden name, not out of bitterness, but because I wanted to be known for my own self and not as the ex Mrs. Jeh Khanna.

I had put my foot down, and requested him to arrange a studio apartment with an independent bathroom and a tiny kitchenette on rent, which I could afford to pay. However I had agreed that it be in a safe neighborhood.

Jeh had offered to pay for a better apartment, but I had refused. He had given me a generous settlement, and I did not want to take any further monetary help from him.

He was going to start a new life with Sonya and I, unlike her, did not want her to be in the same situation, as she had put me in. Once away from Delhi, I was going to cut down my interactions with Jeh to the minimum, except of course, in matters relating to our sons.

Fortunately, they were both adults, and did not need any legal interventions like visitation rights etc.

Our boys too, had been the reason that we had agreed to be more like friends than adversaries, and this sort of comforted them, as they were not torn in their loyalties towards us.

I was to leave for New York by the end of the month; a furnished studio apartment was ready and waiting for me, so much for having an ex who was not only generous but also helpful. I guess we were just not meant to last until death do us apart!

A thought had been rankling in my mind. Should I tell Jeh about Samarthya, incase, if he ever came looking for me, would he give him my address? Finally, I had decided against it, for I felt no such thing was going to happen. Jeh may not like it, because most men can be quite egoistic, when it comes to them being replaced by another man.

Of course, men have no such qualms replacing the woman in their lives with another.

It was exactly five months, twenty days, and looking at his watch, Samarthya calculated, eight hours, thirty minutes and fifteen seconds of painful time since Serena had quietly left the hotel in Cairo and from his life.

Today, he was again at the Delhi airport, waiting to board the same Emirates flight from Delhi to Cairo via Dubai, which was taking him back to Cairo for an official meet. Samarthya recalled the scene, when Serena had tripped on his suitcase.

A smile touched his lips, remembering the indignant look on her flustered face, on finding herself rescued by a stranger and it had not helped, that he had an amused look on his face.

Much as he wanted to deny it, it was at that moment, he had fallen lock stock and barrel for the pretty woman, who was trying to look confident but he had, in an instant, noticed the deep pain in her eyes. He wanted to embrace her there and then, and kiss away the hurt.

They had been fated for each other, because all thru the journey to Cairo, he and Serena had kept bumping in to each other, and finally he had rescued her at the Cairo airport, and realized that they were staying at the same hotel. From then on, much as he wanted to deny his attraction for her, he had been drawn to her, and his life had turned upside down.

Serena had not been like the exotic young beauties he normally dated; in fact she was an exact opposite. She was in her mid forties, closer to him in age, and he liked the fact that though she dressed well, she was not obsessed about being a fashionista.

She had somehow managed, with her simplicity and beauty, to break the hard casing around his heart, which no woman had been able to break, since his marriage to Maheka had fallen apart.

He had resolved that he would never love a woman again, love being a bad word in his dictionary. In spite of that, he had felt like a scum- bag when he had seen the hurt look on Serena's face when he told her that he did not believe in love, and was happy with short affairs, which were merely a means of fulfilling his physical needs.

He had, at once, gone on to assure her that she was precious to him and not just a physical need, a statement that he had not uttered to any woman post Maheka.

S had become jaded and cynical in life, and had forgotten to take pleasures in little things, and Serena had breezed in to his life and made him feel whole again. The trip to the pyramids with her would always hold a special place in his heart, and he had been secretly happy that she had not deleted the one and only photo in which they had posed together.

The picture was a screen saver on his Mac and every -time he switched it on and saw Serena, standing close to him, he felt warmth in his heart that he realized was his love for her.

There was something about Serena, which drew him out of his shell, revealing incidents in his life, which he would have never dreamt of telling anyone. He had ended up sharing the early memories of his growing up in the village, his married life, and the problems with Maheka.

The trip to Abu Simbel had firmly etched Serena in his heart. They had both shared a sizzling physical chemistry; along with a comfort they had in each other's company.

All this, made him sure, that she was the woman with whom he would like to take a chance with happiness, again in life.

Though, he would have felt happier, if Serena would have trusted him enough to reciprocate, by telling her side of the story. He had been astute enough to realize, that though she was married, she was going through a troubled patch because no happily married woman would have ventured alone on a holiday trip. The degree of their relationship showed that they both were looking for some happiness, which was missing in their own lives.

He had decided that before they left Cairo, he would tell Serena that he wanted to spend more time with her in Delhi, hoping she would learn to trust him and share the story of her life with him, and in time fall in love with him, as he had fallen for her.

Samarthya had been tortured with the thoughts, what if Serena had just a temporary fall out with her husband and in a womanly huff had walked off on a holiday trip on her own.

What if he was just a temporary holiday romance, to be forgotten, once she was back in Delhi in the welcoming arms of her husband.

He had been ashamed of himself, for thinking selfishly. Just because he was living a sham of a marriage, did not mean Serena too was experiencing the same. He, almost reluctantly, made himself promise that he would help her salvage her marriage, if there were a chance to do so.

But everything had changed with a calamitous effect. Maheka had brazenly appeared unexpectedly, with her Turkish boyfriend at the Cairo hotel.

She had no shame or concern for Samarthya's feelings, and he too had played the same cards in the past several years. Marriage for them was a mere legal bond, which did not hinder the way they led their personal lives.

Some how on seeing Serena in the hotel lobby, Maheka had intuitively guessed and rightly, that she was special to Samarthya.

She had been so unlike the kind of women Samarthya was normally seen with. Though Maheka had been the cause of her own disastrous marriage, she could not bear to see Samarthya's chance at happiness, and had cattily made it seem to Serena that she was the wronged woman, and her husband played the field with younger and attractive women.

In one shot, she had let Serena know that she was old and not the kind of woman Samarthya normally dated. Also implying, that he was just using Serena, and would dump her once he was bored with her.

Samarthya had known that Serena had been shocked with the whole incident, and even if he had reassured her, it would not have solved matters. Rather than clarifying in the lobby, in front of Maheka, who could have created more mischief for him, he had decided to keep quiet and explain to Serena later on, when he met her alone in the room, which he had been hoping to share with her. After Abu Simbel, he could not bear to be apart from her, when she was so close to him.

But Serena had asked for a separate room, and had refused to open the door to him, despite his many requests. He had left, after telling her that they would speak in the morning and it had come as a shock to him when he discovered that Serena had checked out very early in the morning and also preponed her flight to Delhi.

He had called her desperately many times on her cell phone and the hotel phone but she had refused to return his calls.

He had wanted to rush to the airport, and stop her some how from boarding the flight, but had been constrained by an urgent official meeting that he was supposed to attend in the morning.

So, Serena had left, without giving him a chance to explain his side of the story, that Maheka had deliberately created a rift between the two of them.

On returning from Cairo, he had been upset and angry with Serena, for not having trusted him, and listening to his side of the situation, and he had made no efforts to find her.

He knew the name of her family travel business and could have easily found out her whereabouts, but his ego was hurt that she had just upped and left him, without any clarifications.

After a month, he was secretly disappointed, because he had been hoping that Serena, who had his telephone numbers, would call and speak to him and they would clear all the misunderstandings.

But it seemed to him that he had just been a diversion for Serena, with her going back to her husband and sorting out her issues. She had never shared with him what had plagued her marriage. He had been sure that after Abu Simbel she would have definitely spoken to him about her marriage, but now his mind was besieged with the thoughts that Serena no longer wanted to see him.

All this was taking a toll on his health and work, his colleagues had commented on his weight loss, and his subordinates had been the frequent recipients of his short temper.

In fact his boss had called him to have a chat because he had been so unlike his normal self and suggested that maybe he needed to go on a vacation and unwind. Samarthya knew that he would find peace only when things with Serena had been clarified, about his position in her life.

So, finally, after a few months, he had hired a private investigator to find out, discreetly, Serena's whereabouts and the state of her marriage, because how ever much he loved her, he did not want to upset her married life, if she had gone back to it, and was happy.

The second most crucial decision had been to get Maheka to agree on a divorce. He was clear that he no longer wanted the dead appendage of a marriage around his neck. It had been difficult to get her to talk seriously, as she was some where in South America, with her photographer boyfriend.

She had been very amused on hearing his divorce request, and had ridiculed his choice of Serena as a partner, telling him not to be foolish, and, as always, they should amuse and use their partners and get on with their lives.

She told him it was convenient for them to be married, without any strings attached, leaving them to play the field on their terms, and why did he want to get in to the mess of a real marriage.

"You have been footloose and fancy free for a long time thanks to me! I wonder if you will be interested in that mousy middle aged woman once the novelty has worn off," were Maheka's jibes at him.

"Do her a favor, and leave her, because I don't think any decent looking man has ever looked at her twice! She would think she has received manna from heaven if you chased her," she had laughed cattily.

Samarthya had not wasted his breath refuting her jealous and catty remarks, and had asked her to arrive at an amicable parting, because he knew he would eventually get a divorce with or without Maheka's consent.

Samarthya wanted to be free from Maheka before he met Serena. He was loath that his marriage could in any way hamper what -ever chances he had with her.

Maheka had finally agreed to a mutual divorce, for she was smart in understanding that Samarthya was serious about it, and rather than fighting and wasting money and time, She had accepted a hefty amount for the divorce settlement.

Their daughter Tara had been pretty mature,

Her acceptance of it, showed how deep the rot in their marriage had permeated.

He had shared with Tara his love for Serena and how he wanted to be with her, if she was free, and Tara had been very happy for him wanting to meet Serena.

It was fates' irony that Samarthya's plane was landing at the Delhi airport from Cairo and at the same time Serena was boarding the flight, which was taking her away from Delhi, to New York.

Was fate conjuring that two wonderful people, each oblivious of the other's tremendous love, should never meet? Just when it seemed everything was falling in place, the star- crossed lovers once again part, and we will eagerly wait to see them together again.

Samarthya was in the office and time again looked at the sleek black Rado on his hand, prompting his friend, a senior reporter, to joke if he was on a hot date!

Yes, he wanted to scream; I am finally going to know where I can find the hottest woman in this world, after months of painful parting. But he had merely smiled at him and told him no such luck, just an appointment with the dentist!

The detective from the agency was meeting him in the evening, to give him all the information about Serena. Samarthya was home well before the agent came, and what transpired made him happy, and once again, sad.

The detective had done a thorough job detailing all about Serena's earlier life, and her marriage to Jeh Khanna, and about her two sons, about whom, she had never spoken to him. He was surprised that she was a mother of such older boys, because she was just in her early forties, but then she had married right out of college.

He had felt anger towards Jeh Khanna, for torturing Serena, with his proximity and affair with Sonya, wanting to go smash his face for the pain he had caused her.

But despite this, the report talked of a very amicable relationship between Jeh and Serena post the divorce, and the generous settlement that her ex husband had provided for her.

He had felt a moment of jealousy, and had decided at that moment, that Serena would never have to depend on her ex for her physical well being, and he was going to take care of all her needs.

A hope also raised in his heart, that she was over with her husband, and it would be easier for him to woo her, and win her back again.

He had been pained to hear that she had lost her mother, whom she had loved, and she had borne that painful phase of her life, all alone, except for the support of her college friend Maya. He had mentally thanked Maya for helping his darling to come back to life, deciding one day to go with Serena and thank her personally.

His heart had twisted with pain on reading how Serena had become a recluse and given up on her self, and at the same time swelled with pride in her efforts to become a better person than before.

Then, the detective dropped the bomb shattering all his hopes of finally meeting his dear love. Serena had left just yesterday for New York. Ironically at the same time he was landing in Delhi from Cairo. The detective wanted a couple of weeks or so to find out her where about in New York.

He was confident about an early resolve, because he knew that Serena was surely going to be in touch with her sons, who were studying in a college there. He wanted Samarthya's permission to go ahead with the search, and also advised him that this would incur additional hefty fees.

S had told him not to bother about the expenses, and just get on at the earliest, finding Serena.

Samarthya for the first time in his life felt so lifeless and dejected, just when he had hoped that Serena and he were finally going to meet, they were once again separated.

CHAPTER 13

Serena looked out of the only window in her tiny studio apartment in a Brownstone in Upper West side in New York.

She had been fortunate to get this studio, which overlooked a small patch of green, and had ample sunshine, thus compensating for its small size. The size did not matter to her, because she was not entertaining anyone, except her sons.

It had a comfortable bed, which took almost the whole room and a tiny cul d sac with a bookcase and a table and chair. She had bought a single seat sofa chair, and placed it near the window overlooking the garden patch, and would sit there for hours sometimes, with the sun streaming in thru the glass panes and reflected on her life, which had gone past, and what she would like to do for her future, which looked pretty bare today.

One wall had the closets where she had kept her clothes and bags. She had decided that she would not give in to temptation and buy more clothes, as there was barely any place to keep them.

But maybe, she had grinned to herself, if it was really good she could give in to the enticement.

She and clothes, shoes and bags in that order were synonymous. It must be the childhood deprivation of the same, and then, of course, the woman gene for them was a pretty strong one in her. A shopping expedition was a sure shot way to alleviate the mood for most women.

A barely there kitchenette took care of her meals.

She had decided not to go in for any major cooking expeditions, at present content with take aways, which she would pick on her way back from her long walking sojourns.

Some days she would be happy eating some milk, cereals and fruits and was glad, because if nothing else, New York was helping her shed some more of her unwanted flab.

She wished her bathroom had been a little bigger, having been used to a good sized one at home, which had been her hideaway from the world, when it came down on her with too many problems.

This was tiny compared to it, but neat and comfortable, with a spacious closet on one wall, to hold her precious shoes and toiletries.

So, here she was, almost fifteen days in to New York. Her sons had come and met her in the first week, giving her helpful tips around the city. It had not been very stressful for her, as she had been here earlier also, on many occasions.

She was missing them because they had gone back for their spring break to India, right after settling her in, and would be back in a fortnight.

They probably would not have gone back to India and stayed back for her, except Jeh was getting married to Sonya, and they were obviously expected to be there. Though I no longer loved Jeh, there was still a tiny corner of my heart devoted to our memories, and the love we had shared. It had hurt a little, that Jeh had so easily moved on in life.

Not like me, I was miserable without Samarthya, my thoughts constantly about him.

I wondered if I could gather the courage and call him but then I was a coward, I had run away from taking a chance with Samarthya, unable to bear rejection once again in life.

I thought it was better this way, loving him one-sided from a distance. Some how my elder son's adage "no pain, no gain," did not apply for me here. I had all the pain and no gain!

The fortnight the boys were away, I simply did not do much, having already done the sightseeing of all the museums and other landmarks on my earlier trips. I would just walk a lot, sometimes for hours and generally see the world go by. I was finally firming up with the idea that I would study further for a Masters in History with a special interest in archaeology. I guess it's never too late in life, if one really desires to do something.

I would have to sit for the necessary exams, and it had been a long time since I had left studies. For many evenings I was glued to my computer, researching about the universities and their requirements. Initially I was daunted by the amount of studies required, but I was not the one to give up easily. I embarked on my new mission with a lot of determination and prepared my study schedules. I wanted to be able to apply to colleges by the fall and I really had a lot of things on my plate.

Now, I did not know how my day went by, I had barely time to think or do anything except my studies and my daily chores.

It was only in the night, when I lay on the bed tired and mentally sapped, my thoughts would veer off to Samarthya. While In Abu Simbel, I had thought we had shared something beautiful and probably we could have a future together. I had also decided to share with him all about my troubled marriage and how I had decided that I would go back and ask Jeh for a divorce.

But the Cairo episode in the hotel had broken my heart. His wife, Maheka's remarks had made me face up the very doubts I had tried to suppress. How could such a handsome and sexy man have been attracted towards me? Agreed, I was no beauty queen and had pleasing looks, but then, age was not on my side. Samarthya had got over the novelty of romancing a woman, who was not the usual exotic young ones he dated, as Maheka had drawled.

Even today an older man can easily get a woman, who is old enough to be his daughter, and society will still accept the sugar daddies with an indulgence of men and their needs, and, of course, money can buy anything for men.

But, for most women, age becomes a barrier when looking for a suitable partner. If older women, who are beautiful and have the money and position in society, have younger handsome companions, they are called cougars with some degree of derision.

Society was unfair, always biased towards men but hopefully things were changing. The very fact that I have been bold enough to opt out of a dead marriage, and also on top of it, had indulged in a holiday romance, is something to do with the change of the mindsets of women today.

We are clearer in our needs' and wants' and do not hesitate to work towards them.

My days were spent studying, and the nights in endless hours, pining for S, who despite my efforts to forget him, seemed to plough deeper in my heart.

All this was starting to take a toll. My face looked almost gaunt, and I think, I had lost a couple of more kilos in weight. At another time, I would have been dancing in joy, but not now. It was a realization of my failure to take charge of my life, and once again, I was letting a man who did not want me, control it.

I told myself to forget him, and maybe have a fling with a total stranger, and get a grip on my life. I knew I was thinking foolish, it was not a physical need that I was seeking, but was missing the easy companionship and mental connect I had with him.

My sons were back in New York, and they were coming over to see me in the evening, and I was extremely happy to see my darlings and share with them all that I had done, and my study plans for the future.

Samarthya was elated. The detective agency had finally found Serena's whereabouts.

There had been a delay of over a fortnight in finding her since she had left, because her sons had come back for their father's wedding.

He had applied for a month long leave from office which had been readily granted by his boss, who had been after him to take a break.

He still could not believe that on the coming weekend he would be standing outside Serena's apartment. He did not want to call her, but give her a surprise.

On the long flight to New York, S was elated; yet, sometimes doubts crept in his mind, what if Serena did not want him. What if she still loved her husband, and he had been, a one off fling to take her mind off her traumatic marriage. Moreover, she had never made any effort to contact him. He had pushed the thoughts aside, waiting to see Serena personally and asking her if she wanted him as much as he wanted her.

It was a beautifully sunny day, and Serena and the boys, who did not have classes on a Saturday, had decided to picnic in the Central Park.

Every time she had passed the park she had been assailed by feelings of loneliness, seeing happy families, groups of friends or lovers hand in hand enjoying the beauty of the Park, which was like a green oases in the middle of a concrete jungle of buildings. At those moments, she had sometimes imagined, what it would be like to walk in the park with Samarthya by her side. He would kiss her passionately, without any cultural barriers, which impeded such public display of affection in India.

Those had been futile thoughts, and they had pained Serena.

Today, She was with her sons after a long time, and they had avoided the topic of Jeh's wedding, to spare her any feelings of pain.

But she had been pretty fine with it, and even asked them about it, and all that had happened. She had been glad that Sonya had not shown any bias towards her sons, and had accepted them as part of Jeh's life.

Jeh had assured me that his marriage to Sonya would in no way affect the future of our sons. He had confided that neither he nor Sonya were interested in having any children.

My sons were secure financially, as well as mentally. They were grown up and mature enough to have accepted our divorce and the presence of others in their parents' lives.

I had wondered, many times, whether they would have accepted Samarthya's presence in my life, as readily as they had accepted Sonya?

I never had to think much, as the possibility of it happening would never arise.

The day was wonderful, and after a long walk in the park, to burn off the humungous amount of food that my sons had bought and we had eaten, they dropped me at the apartment.

It was still early evening, and they had plans to party, as any young boys their age would, on a weekend. They were sweet and caring, making sure that I did not feel lonely. I was touched and my heart burst with love to see my little men making me feel like a Queen. What would I have done with out them, I could not even imagine!

Reena Puri

After they had left, I had a quick hot shower, to wash off the sweat and tiredness of the day, deciding to relax by watching a television show and skip on my studies for the day. I changed in to my old comfortable floral shorts and a tee, planning to call in an early night, after watching the show.

It was seven and I was almost drooping off to sleep when the doorbell rang. I did not know anyone in New York and all I could think was that maybe my sons had come back for something, but they would have called me, and so feeling a little nervous, I first fixed the security latch on the door before deciding to open it.

The concierge, for the brownstone had left early that day, otherwise normally he always called on the intercom, before letting any visitor in.

I had nervously called out who was it and when I heard the quiet reply; the earth seemed to have moved beneath my feet. I had to hold on to the door to steady myself, unable to believe that it was he on the other side of the door.

"Is that You?" I had almost squeaked, my voice as if strangled.

"Yes it's me."

"Are we going to talk behind closed doors or will you let me in, darling?" Samarthya asked me in an indulgent tone.

I had opened the door, forgetting that it was on the security latch, and it opened partially, and I saw him. My whole body went in a shock, I just did not know how to react, and stood there like a zombie, unable to react.

Samarthya reached out to me thru the small opening and gently touched my cheek, "Darling, will you not let me in?"

The touch of his hand on my skin was like a bolt from the blue and I shook myself out of the shock and hastily scrambled to unlock the door.

There he was, my handsome tormentor, standing before me in flesh and blood. I reached out, as if in a trance, to touch him, wanting to make sure that I was not dreaming.

My fingers gently touching those deep sexy enigmatic eyes, which had me, totally bowled over him and then moving down to run over the handsome face, which seemed leaner and tired.

Suddenly his hand snaked out and held my hand captive and then still looking at me with those to-die for sexy eyes, started kissing each finger of my hand slowly.

Unable to bear the sweet torture I had pulled my hand away and had just rushed into his arms, sobbing with tears running freely down my cheeks. Samarthya had gathered me tight in his arms crying out, "Yes, my bebo, Yes, my darling I am here"! He had come in, and shut the door to the tiny apartment. Then, as if a river of passion had broken all its dams, We were tearing at each other, crying out incoherent words of endearments, berating each other and I was almost beating his broad chest with my fists and crying at the same time.

Samarthya had just held my hands captive and swooped down on my lips and all sounds had seized in that small room except for two writhing bodies straining to get as close to each other as was humanly possible.

We could barely breath, and broke off from our torrid kiss, to gulp air, like two people who were on the verge of drowning.

I was feeling faint with the rush of emotions, and I just fell back on the bed, pulling S along with me, and for some time we both just lay there breathing hard, till we had calmed down a bit.

I rolled and lay half over Samarthya, still unable to believe that he was really there, dropping tiny kisses on his temple, his eyes, his nose and lips as if seeking to reaffirm that it was he, and I was not dreaming.

S gently rolled over me, his hard body, trapping mine from head to toe, as if reassuring me that it was him, and his lips kissing every inch of my face, and my hands feverishly exploring the knotted muscles of his back.

I was impatient, I wanted to feel the warm silk of his skin and tugged impatiently at his tee shirt, helping S pull it over his head. S, had with one flick, pulled off my flimsy tee, and then my shorts, and I lay there naked on the bed, watching with fevered eyes, S divest his jeans impatiently and his skimpy slinky underwear.

I just held out my arms, with S reaching out, and pinning me underneath his hard body.

We made fast and furious love, our bodies had been starved, and the burning hunger had to be assuaged. There were no words exchanged just the primeval mating of a man and a woman, who had been without each other for a long time.

Sometimes later, we were finally spent of the overwhelming passion, which had struck us.

"Serena, I wish you had not disappeared from Cairo, without giving me a chance to explain. I had been very angry with you and had at that point, decided that I was better of without you, if you did not trust me," said Samarthya.

I had placed my fingers on his lips, begging for forgiveness, and the pain that we had both endured. I explained to him that I had been unclear about my own marriage, and the episode with his wife had freaked me out. I had once again felt betrayed, and had bolted from the scene, that being the only way I could cope with the hurt and pain.

I told him I loved him so much that it hurt, and in all these months there was not a single day, when I had not thought of him. So many times I had been tempted to call him, but would give up, thinking that I had been just a holiday romance for him, and he did not want anything more from me.

It was almost mid-night, S and I had been catching up on the past six months of our lives, finally realizing that we were famished. I had gone to my kitchenette to make some eggs and toast for us, and S had come in that tiny space, and distracted me by kissing the back of my neck, knowing well, how aroused I became when he did that. I had laughingly teased him that he would have to go hungry, if he did any more of that.

S had whispered in my ears that he was hungry for my body, and he would starve if I did not give it to him, and to f... the food.

I was brimming with happiness and a womanly pride, that I had my man, who not only desired me, but also loved me as much, as I did him. After satiating our stomachs, S had picked me and had sat with me on his lap on the sofa chair by the window, and told me all about his divorce from Maheka, that had come through recently.

"Darling, now that we are both free from our pasts, I think we should decide on our future without any more delay."

"I cannot bear to spend another day without you, now that I have found you," said Samarthya.

I told him that I echoed his sentiments but it was not that simple and that I would need to tell my sons about us. I was a little wary and hesitant, as to how they would react to my having a new man in my life.

"If they have accepted another woman as a step-mother, why should they not accept your having another man in your life. I hope they don't expect you to lead a life of virtuous motherhood," remarked S sarcastically.

I hit at him, telling him that was not so, my boys were pretty broad –minded, and that the fear was in my mind. I had messed up my marriage because of my insecurities. What if it happened again?

Marriage was something I could not contemplate. I was not ready to give him my hundred percent, and that would not be fair on my part.

S had been irritated, unable to understand my doubts. He said that we were more than physically compatible in bed, and we both loved and wanted to be with each other, so where was the question of confusion in my mind. He was clear that he wanted me twenty-four seven in his life and without me, his life would come to a standstill.

I understood his point but told him, that I needed time before committing myself to another relationship. I did not want to rush in haste and repent later for the next twenty years. This time I would not be able to face an end to another tumultuous marriage.

S had got up and led me to the bed saying
"Let's talk about this tomorrow, right now I have a need that I am sure you also have, and are not going to deny"!

This time we had made love gently, exploring each and every inch of our bodies. It seemed like Samarthya was worshipping me, trying to wipe away my fears, and promising to love me always.

My heart swelled with infinite love for him, I wondered whether it was humanly possible for some one to love as much as I did him.

He had taken me to the moon, and with a shattering climax, both of us had crashed to the earth, holding on to, and crying out our love for each other.

It was late morning when I woke up to find myself in the protective circle of Samarthya's arms. My face almost buried in his chest, I loved the musky odor of his warm skin, and gave in to the temptation of licking it with my tongue.

"Woman, if you are ready to face the consequences, then go on with it," S had drawled sleepily and had pulled me closer to his body, letting me feel the extent of his arousal.

It was much later when we finally got up. We were still starving for each other and could not seem to have a fill of the other. Samarthya had laughed and said he was doing pretty fine for his age, and I had blushed after a long time. He always managed to get under my skin.

The next few days, Samarthya and I had done nothing much than just going out for meals, and making love, in the order that was convenient to us. I knew, soon, I would have to meet my sons and tell them, before they came to the apartment and met Samarthya.

The following weekend I called, and arranged to meet them first, and then later on, depending on how it took off, I would get them to meet S.

Surprisingly, much to my relief, my sons were both very happy to know that I had found love in my life, and were most keen to meet S and that same evening we had all met for dinner in a Thai restaurant, off Broadway.

The boys and S had got along from the word go.

He had treated them as mature adults, and they had accorded him the respect that a parent commanded, leaving me brimming with pride at the wonderful men in my life.

It had been very crucial for me that my sons accept Samarthya, because I did not want to start a new life by making them unhappy, and their happiness was more important. I guess we mothers are such creatures, our children's well being, the most important for us.

Samarthya had joked with me and asked what if Atharv and Adiraj had been against our relationship, would I have left him?

The very thought of that terrified me, but fortunately, God had been kind to me and spared me the torture of having to take that decision.

S had persisted, wanting to know the answer just for the sake of knowing, and I had laughed and said that I would have had a clandestine relationship with him, if he had agreed.

"For you, darling, I would have begged and won over your sons, because I love you and want the world to know that you are my woman, so the question of a clandestine affair does not arise," said Samarthya. Despite things working out as far as my sons were concerned, I was still wary of a permanent commitment to Samarthya. I had barely achieved independence, which I now wanted to relish, even though I desired and loved Samarthya, and wanted to be with him.

I was learning to live a life without any dependence on anyone for my personal happiness, and wanted to prove to myself that I could lead a life on my own. I did not want love to be my sole criteria for happiness.

Today I had taken Samarthya to Central Park; there had been this underlying desire to be like the lovers whom I had secretly envied. I did not care that we were the minority amongst them, as in being much older. But then, when did love see any physical barriers like age or color of skin or religion.

If it happens, we should just flow along with it. We walked hand in hand in the Park, on a bright sunny afternoon. I felt downright sexy and desired, when S kissed me passionately, amongst people who were as oblivious to us as we were to them.

Samarthya had once again raised the topic of what we planned to do next, because he was only on a month long vacation and that was soon coming to an end. He wanted me to go back with him to Delhi and then decide to get married at the earliest.

On reaching back to the apartment and after an early dinner, I had shared with S my desire to study further, which would take the next two years of my life and I told him that it would mean I was not ready to take on the added commitment of a marriage and the ensuing responsibilities that came along with it. We had barely known each other except that we were extremely compatible physically but living together day in and day out as a married couple was another ball game.

I reasoned with him that the relationship of lovers some how changes when they get married, and the expectation levels get skewed and that's when the troubles start.

I did not want any thing to screw up my happiness with him and was willing to wait for my studies to get over. I asked S if he was agreeable to my plan.

Samarthya was ok with my study bit but not at all happy with my plan to pursue them here, for it meant that we would be separated for a long time, and that was unacceptable to him.

He argued why could I not pursue my studies in India, that way we both could be in Delhi, and he joked, he would be the most pliable and cooperative husband I could ever hope for.

That exactly was what I was fighting for; I did not want to sacrifice my desires for the people I loved. I wanted them to accept me as I was.

For the first time, S and I had a serious discord, and he asked me sarcastically whether he should leave the next day, incase he was being a barrier to my plans and maybe I really did not want or love him.

I had cried that night and told him he was being unfair, because he knew how much I loved him, and every day away from him would be as painful to me, and that I just wanted to do something for myself, for once.

"Why can't you come and just stay with me in New York as a live in partner?" I had asked him tearfully.

There had been a period of quiet, before S had lashed out to me, "Serena, you do not want to marry me, that means only one thing, either you don't love me or you don't trust me and I am hurt now."

I had rushed to S, crying out that he was not at fault. It was I who was all messed up in my mind after a failed marriage and needed time, to make another commitment, which this time I wanted desperately for keeps, because I was madly in love with him.

We could live together for some time, like six months or more, and then decide if we both wanted a marriage. I would be the happiest woman if that were to happen.

S had not been very happy, and that night his lovemaking had reflected his emotions, for the first time he had just taken me without any tender foreplay and rolled over to sleep on his side of the bed.

I had understood his anger, because here was a man who loved me, and wanted to marry me, and I was asking him to wait and share a live in relationship.

The next few days before Samarthya was leaving were fraught with tension. I did not have the courage to ask S for his opinion on the option I had asked. Finally, on the day he was leaving, all he had said was that he would think about it and let me know.

CHAPTER 14

Amonth had passed since Samarthya had gone back to Delhi, and I had not heard from him. I was miserable, knowing that it was because of my own doings, but at the same time I wanted to live my life for my own self too.

I had called him once, but he had said he was busy and would call me back, but he never did.

I was once again limping back to life. My sons had asked me about S, and I had been very upfront with them, that I did not want a commitment of a marriage for some time, and that had not been acceptable to S.

I wondered what my sons must have thought about their mother in a live in relationship, but I did not care, as long as it did not hurt anyone else, my life was mine to do as I wished. This was a liberal society and I could take a chance here, unlike in India, where such a thing was still a taboo, especially for people our age.

I had got up to a gloomy morning, with dark overcast skies, and by the time I got over with my classes, (Yes I finally had secured an admission for my Masters in History) and rushed to the tube station to go back home, it was pouring in earnest.

I was almost soaked, the umbrella no match for the downpour. I was fumbling for the key in my copious bag, and trying to hold on to the umbrella at the same time.

"Lady, do you need any help?"

I almost jumped with joy on hearing the familiar drawl of my beloved nemesis.

Turning back I saw it was he, his familiar silver grey locks soaking wet, and I just flew into his arms, my umbrella tumbled off in the wind and my bag ditched on the pavement.

There we stood in the rain, holding each other, our lips fused, the rain mingling with our tears of joy.

The passing pedestrians looked at the middle- aged couple that was locked in a passionate embrace in the pouring rain, with indulgent smiles. Some clapped when the handsome man picked up the bag and with one sweep bellying his age swooped the pretty woman and walked off towards happiness.

Printed in the United States
By Bookmasters